# Jane and the Fighting Quoins

## The Beginning

R. Anthony Gehrig

Creative Gaming Revolution, LLC

R. Anthony Gehrig

Jane and the Fighting Quoins: The Beginning



Cover art by Phillip Chauncey

Published by Creative Gaming Revolution, LLC

www.cgrdigital.com

# My Deepest Thanks

Phillip Chauncey: Thank you for your cover art! A book often needs to dress well to get the attention of potential readers. Your cover art should do just that. I know dealing with someone as obsessive as I am, especially with the details, can be trying. Still, I cannot express enough gratitude for the time and effort you put into this original piece of art!

I also want to thank you for the years of gameplay and work you have contributed to Glory and Power's creation, the world these stories are based in. As of this point, that name may not be final, but this world is profoundly shaped by you and the hours and years you have put in. It has been a great time. Hopefully, it will continue on into future projects and into the planned future stories for Jane and Paden.

Christopher Rohan, Daniel Yates, Craig Florentine, and Johnathan Cintron: Each of you as well have made this world alive. Each game we played put a brick on the foundation as we built Glory and Power from the mazes I created in 10th grade to a fully realized and fleshed out world. Though it has been decades since we could get together and have a long game session, those past games live on in memory, and on occasion, you will see them shine through as I work through this series. Thank you!

To my parents: I am finally trying to do something from my kingdom on cloud nine! I know it has been a long time coming, but we always knew I would try this path. Thank you for allowing us those endless weekends with my friends crowding around the den as we played countless hours of the 'nerd game.' Writing these stories would never have happened without your willingness to let us dream and create! Thank you!

To my wife: It is your turn to deal with me and my eccentric behavior. You may still not fully realize what exactly you have gotten yourself into even after all these years, but you let me be me, and that is the key. You may never read my stories. I know it is not your thing. But I appreciate all the other things you do for me and your support as I go down this path. Thank you!

To my kids: I don't know if any of you will ever read this, but every writer knows that his words can often speak volumes about his character, his beliefs, and his values. May you see a bit of me in these writings. May it bring you pride to see your father's written thoughts and stories. You bring me joy, and that joy helps me write, and for that, I thank you!

And to you, my reader: To you, I owe my most humble thanks. You are now also a part of this world. A world built by family and friends finally coming out to be shared into your lives. May you love it as much as we have!

Table of Contents

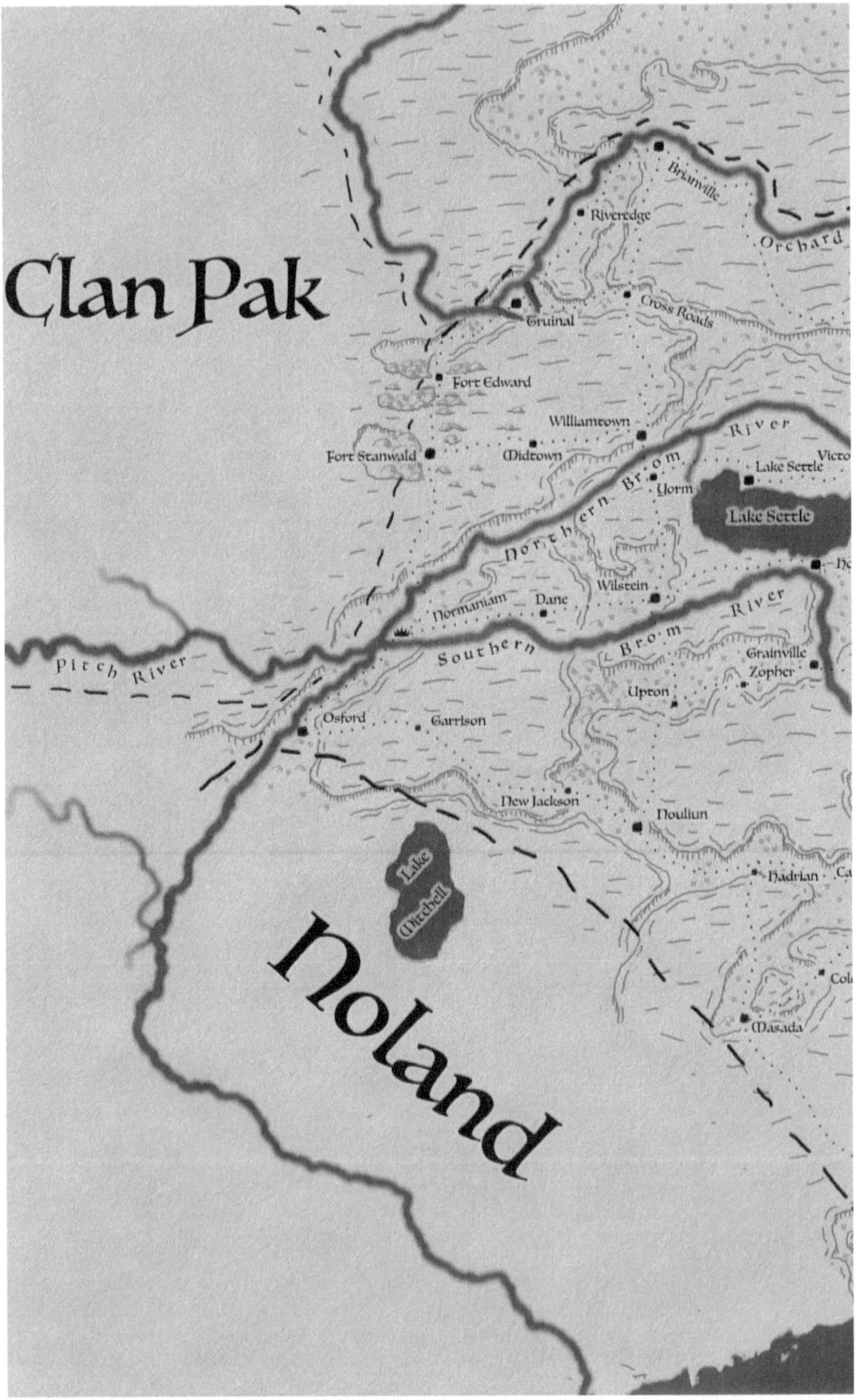

Clan Pak

Brianville

Riveredge

Orchard

Gruinal

Cross Roads

Fort Edward

Williamtown

Fort Stanwald

Midtown

River

Lake Settle

Yorm

Lake Settle

Northern Brom

Wilstein

Normaniam

Dane

River

Southern

Brom

Pitch River

Grainville

Zopher

Upton

Osford

Garrison

New Jackson

Noulun

Lake Mitchell

Hadrian

Noland

Masada

Sandsted
River Orchard
Wavecrest
River
Northtown
Jacksons
Myerston
Shellfish Cove
Workshire
Jensen
Killveran
Hamsted
Pat's Forest
Reden
Efficax
Oak Field
Hampton
East Port
Dublin
Ackerman
Berlial
Fallow
Port Calindia
Ingleton
Amerson
Durin
Versalas
Lincoln
Ahunum
Teuto
Vetera
Narbo
Epirus
Hempetius
Marshall
Blackport
Newport

*Story 1*

# *The Relics of the Sun*

I will never forget the day I met Jane. On that particular day, several Relics of the Sun were in the city of Normandia in possession of the Captain of the guard, Joshua Berkley. Now, I realize most people in Broma know about the Relics of the Sun; but for outsiders who do not, I will devote a moment to explaining them.

In the country of Broma, where most of my adventures with Jane took place, there are a series of magical doors. These doors allow a good person to step through, transporting that person to another location instantly. However, there is a limitation to these doors as they do not allow evil to pass through them. Evil not being able to pass through is where the Relics come into play.

If an evil man has a Relic in his possession, it will allow him to pass through the doors. Allowing a wicked man to pass through the doors may seem like a strange thing to allow, but there are times when prisoners need to be transported across the country quickly. The guards can give a Relic to the criminal and walk through with him to their new destination. Upon arrival, the guards must take the relic from the criminal for safekeeping.

When not in use, the Relics of the Sun are kept in a vault in Fort Ray, though sometimes travel is required to bring them to where they are needed. Traveling with the relic poses many dangers for the guards. Once away from the doors, the relics are vulnerable. Thus, moving the Relics in this manner can provide criminals ample opportunities for stealing the Relics. An example of this occurred on the day I met Jane.

As I started my walk in Normandia, I had no idea the Relics were in town. The day was cloudy and colder than expected, even for the month of Nivalis in southern Broma. Though still not cold enough to snow, it made a man want to find a nice inn, hot tea, and the sight of a lovely barmaid. Unfortunately, I had to endure it because I had to work.

As a Duelist of the Fighter's Guild, I was endeavoring to start my very own group. You see, I had been working for Oswald Kirk, a Thane in the Guild. Upon Ozzy's retirement, he gave each of his men a sum of money to hire their very own men. With youth's eagerness, I set out to hire the most skillful warriors and make a name for myself. Sadly, I had been trying for weeks without any luck. I knew it was because of my low rank and perceived lack of experience, but I had not given up hope.

With that in mind, I begged Ozzy for a recommendation. Since he had seen proof of my worth many times before, he could vouch for my leadership qualities. Besides, we also had a strong relationship outside of work. Therefore, he gave me a letter of recommendation, but it did come with advice. He suggested that I work some solo cases in the city first. A reputation could be the key to my goal, and I was ready to try anything to start my group.

I found myself walking from Ozzy's new estate in the Stone District of Normandia to the Market District, where the Fighter's Guild kept residency. I thought about taking a taxi cart, but my eagerness and energy made walking more pleasant than riding. The letter in my hand made the day feel good despite the cold. I was so excited that I even hummed an old drinking song as I walked along.

The vast stone building of the local Guild was only twenty blocks away, so I arrived quickly. Normandia had been the seat of the Fighter's Guild for almost two hundred years. The building's grandeur reflected its importance to the country as Dwarves and Mages had built it at great expense, leaving no details overlooked. They had sealed all the seams with magic, which made the whole building one big piece of stone that appeared to have grown from the ground. Facilities such as these were the most impressive building style in the world, and once set like this, few things could harm such a structure.

It was a beautiful building with two high steeples and

a considerable stone overhang with Amoran columns. The marble stairs led to huge red doors carved with scenes of warriors fighting a dragon. The majesty of the building was so impressive that I stopped and stared for a few moments imagining the work that would be needed to complete such a structure. A cool breeze shook me out of my thoughts and brought me back to the mission at hand, and I made my way into the Fighters' Guild.

The building was just as remarkable on the inside as it was on the outside. It housed training rooms and a bar and inn. Yet I didn't want to get distracted. I went directly to the recruiting area where willing workers would enlist for positions. Young adults would apply for membership within the Guild. As it was the winter season, most had met their responsibilities on the farm, eager to find adventures. If they were lucky, they might find a new career. If not, they would be in the fields again in the spring. Because of this, I was hoping I would find a few willing to work for a novice leader.

The man behind the counter was Gregory, a Fighters' Guild Elite and recruiter.

"What can I do for you today, Paden?" the man asked me with a weary groan.

This trip was my fifth in two days, and I was sure he was getting tired of me. Gregory was a short man but broad like a bear. He had a large hooked nose and dark beady eyes, but his smile was pleasant, and his salt and pepper hair gave him a fatherly look.

"I am looking to see if I have had any luck today, and I would like to upgrade my resume with this recommendation," I said as I handed him the letter from Ozzy and my fighter's tags. He looked at it, and his eyebrows rose at the sight of Ozzy's name. As a Thane, Ozzy rank made him a tier four Guild member, and that was impressive. After all, there are only five tiers. Still, my level was that of Duelist, and as a tier two, Greg warned me not to get my hopes set too high.

"It's a good time of the year to recruit, son," Gregory said as he took out a quill and my scroll, "but we have had over fifteen people advertise, and you are the only one below the rank of Brawler. There are many leaders and not enough followers."

He then looked me in the eye and returned both the letter and my tags, saying, "Son, a word of advice. Work for the groups a few more years and try again when you reach Brawler rank. I know you are eager and probably capable, but few people will start with someone of such low ranking, and those that will are not usually worth it."

Of course, my blood boiled at the audacity of being told didn't have enough experience, but I knew, deep down, he was right. It would be a long shot with so many competitors around, and there was nothing I could do but hope for the best.

I left the Guild with an advertisement laid out and hoped that the name of the Thane "Ozzy" Kirk and his recommendation would be enough to land me a few good men. Yet, deep down, I knew the truth. Most would see me as too young, too inexperienced. My enthusiasm had wained. I now felt like I would have to take the advice of the old man. I didn't like the idea of being a grunt again and taking orders from someone else.

In my sad state, I yearned for cold ale or the warmth of whiskey. The urge was strong enough that I had to fight it down. I had vowed to no longer touch that stuff, so I looked around for a distraction and saw the Cathedral's steeple a few blocks away. Its architecture was more conventional than the Fighters' Guild but was no less grand. I decided to head over and get my mind off the disappointing words of the Fighter's Guild Elite.

The walk felt much colder than it had before. Most likely, this only due to my mood, but it didn't make the effect any less real. I had started to shiver by the time I reached the Cathedral and was looking forward to going inside and seeing the stonework. It was a large building with a huge stain glass window and a steeple that reached so far into the sky that it seemed to pierce the heavens. But at that moment, none of it caught my attention.

There she was. I knew then that I would remember that moment forever because sitting on a small, painted mustang sat a woman of incredible beauty. She was gowned in a suit of mail listening to a Grand Protector. Even if I had known what she would mean to me and my future, my heart could not have raced any faster.

Her frame was slender, but even under the mail's box-like shape, she displayed the hourglass figure that all women want, yet few can achieve. Her hair was dark with a bluish hue, her sun-kissed skin had a healthy glow, and her eyes were like two sparkling emeralds. But it was her leg that caught my attention the most. She was gowned like a Paladin, a lower-ranking Warrior of God, and had chosen a medium length riding skirt adorned with the church's symbols. It had a high split that showed off her long tanned leg, suggestive of what was beyond. I stood transfixed.

I was still staring when she turned for a look around and noticed my eyes. I caught a quick blush as she grabbed her skirt and adjusted it, but to no avail. The skirt was designed for movement and would never conceal the leg when riding. Still, it didn't show anything more than her thigh and did ensure her modesty. However, to a hot-blooded man, that is often all it takes to blush.

She must have realized the futility of the situation but seeing my embarrassment was enough for her to relax. Even so, she kept a hand on her skirt just in case. So, to avoid further embarrassment, I turned to walk past and pretended to look at the building. It was then that I heard their conversation for the first time.

“You are to get a member of the Guild to go with you, Jane. It will not do to have a Paladin cut down in the street,” the Grand Protector was saying as I walked past them. His voice was stern but gentle, and I realized he was worried about her well being.

“I understand Henry, but I don’t have a lot of time,” she argued. At the sound of raised voices, the horse whinnied, so she leaned forward and stroked the mustang’s head. Her voice was clear and fit her beauty perfectly. It had an almost soothing quality to it even though she was arguing. It gave me the impression of class and was a tease to her wealthy upbringing.

“Then we will need to find someone quickly,” I heard Henry say. I was looking at the Cathedral’s cornerstone listening to them talk for a reason I cannot explain to this day. The stone was smooth and cut evenly, and the chisel marks were only visible to a trained eye like mine. It was delicate work and showed that the stonemason was a true master. I had almost managed to lose myself in thought when I heard Henry say, “What about that gentleman behind me?”

I had started walking towards the entrance before I realized he had been talking about me. I turned around and found they were both looking my way. I was a little taken aback and froze while I thought of what I wanted to say. I knew it wasn't an excellent example of leadership, but she had me flustered. She was examining me with a cold, clear, intelligent gaze and those, 'fall into lovely,' emerald eyes. She seemed to be mulling over whether I would be of any use to her, and it made me nervous.

Henry's expression was more pensive, much like Ozzy would get when he made up his mind. "Yes, Fighters' Guild by dress and ranked in the second tier," he said to himself. "I take it, you normally use a spear?" This question was more of a statement. I didn't even get a chance to answer when he continued talking to Jane. "I believe God sent this one to you, and I believe he will do nicely. Besides, I don't think he will say no to the proposition."

I looked at him with amazement. I had worked with Paladins and Priests before. They were an odd sort and used magic I didn't begin to understand. So it was not strange for them to know things the rest of the world did not. However, this was one of the most impressive displays I had seen by any of them. I wondered how he had guessed so much, seeing only my appearance.

"He looks strong, but I would like a recommendation from the Guild before I say yes, Henry," Jane said in a cold voice.

"Son, what is your name?" Henry asked as he walked

towards me.

“Paden, sir,” I said as I handed him my recommendation from Ozzy. I don’t know what made me do it, but I felt as compelled to show it to him as I had to Gregory at the Fighters’ Guild.

“About that recommendation, Jane, he seems to have one that I can vouch for,” he said as he looked at the letter with a smile. “Paden, leader of the Fighting Quoins, and recommended by Ozzy. How is that old rascal?” he asked.

I was a little surprised that he knew Ozzy, but it also made me a little more relaxed. “Very well, Father,” I said with a smile. I had finally collected myself and wanted to make the best showing I could. There was a possible opportunity here, and I didn’t want to miss it. “He just retired and moved to the Stone District.”

The Grand Protector smiled even broader as he handed the letter back. “He is a good man. I should visit him now that he is a full-time resident.”

“He would like that a lot, I am sure,” I replied, but my mind quickly turned to business because I needed to know what the mission would involve. Paladins fought things that others would turn white with fear from, and though I am no coward, there are things best, not tempted. So I asked, “What is the job you have in mind, Father?”

“Just Henry, son,” the Grand Protector said as he motioned me towards Jane, who was sitting there patiently. “Let the Priests hold to pomp and ceremony. I prefer the name my parents chose.”

“My apologies Henry,” I said as I walked over to stand beside Jane and her painted horse.

“You never have to apologize for being polite,” Henry replied, still with a friendly smile. “But as to the matter at hand, let me be frank because I know I can trust you.” I wasn’t sure how he could be so sure, but I wasn’t going to argue. “I have been charged with protecting some relics that have come into the possession of Guard Captain Joshua Bentley and his guards. They are transporting several prisoners through Hegrig’s Castle tomorrow to Efficax to stand trial for the crimes of murder in Reden.”

“The Relics of the Sun,” I stated as my mind quickly came to the right conclusion.

“Most defiantly,” Henry replied. “As you know, the relic will allow them to pass through the holy doors under that castle. However, it has come to our attention that several members of the thieves’ Guild have arrived. How they got tipped off is not known, but they are on the scent. If they were to get these relics, they could use our very own transports for evil purposes.”

I was listening intently to the conversation with only an occasional glance at Jane. She seemed bored as she scanned the crowd, but at the mention of the relics, her eyebrows shot up ever so slightly. It was evident that even if the Grand Protector somehow trusted me, she did not.

"Jane here is supposed to trail Vance. He is a thief we happen to know is in the city and believe he is part of the gang. He is staying at an inn called the White Doe in Baker's district, and we suspect he will meet with the rest of them later today. Once we know that location, we will send in the guard and stop any theft attempts on the Relics before they start. I want you to assist her, and I can make a gold coin your reward."

I looked at the Guardian with interest. Everyone in Broma knew of the Relics of the Sun. However, the guards guarded then fiercely that few had ever seen them, unless, of course, you were a prisoner in transport. This mission was serious stuff, and I realized the implications. Such an important task could help my credit, not to mention the ten silver worth of gold. I also was very good at observation, and it was an odd man who could escape my notice. This mission seemed like the right kind of task for me and would at least keep me busy while I waited for news from the Guild.

"I accept," I said as I shook Henry's hand. "I take it we start now?"

"Yes." He said as he returned my handshake warmly. His grip was firm and warm and made me feel accepted. This man was the kind of guy I had made my meager carrier around and the type of man I could inspire to be. I was glad of this opportunity and distraction and felt a tinge of confidence that this could at least get my name out there. “I will expect the two of you to leave right away. The sooner we can watch or mark, the faster we can end this problem. What do you need?”

“My ax is back at Ozzy’s house. It will take a little while to go get it,” I answered, cursing myself for not leaving the house prepared. I knew better than to go out of the house unarmed.

“Not a spearman?” He mused as he stepped back. “I could have sworn by the calluses on both hands. Is it a big ax?” It dawned on me how he had guessed my occupation so easily. My dress consisted of a travelers cloak with a broad sword buckle. I had on two steal bracers near my wrists, and calluses covered my hand. Henry hadn’t used magic to guess anything about me, and I felt a bit mad at myself for not catching on to it earlier.

“No, it’s normally a spear, Henry,” I confirmed with a laugh and a slap on the back. “But it is too obvious for the city. I have learned that a small weapon is sometimes necessary for discretion.”

He smiled wide as I had confirmed his guess. I learned later that it was a bit of a game for him to guess other’s occupations. I also would come to find out that he was very good at it. “Well, if it is an ax you need, I can provide you one without hesitation, but I will need it back.” With that, he turned and motioned for a squire who had been standing near the cathedral doors. The squire ran inside quickly and appeared a few moments later with a war ax. It had a moon blade, ash shaft and looked pretty functional.

As I accepted the weapon, it dawned on me that I would be a grunt again. This mission would be Jane’s, so I would be acting as a second. However, for some reason taking orders from Jane did not seem like an alarming prospect. Besides, at that time, I figured it was a one-time deal. Little did I know how wrong that thought was.

“Well, you are in charge, Jane. What would you like me to do?” I asked with a sincere smile. I thought at the time that I had put a bit too much charm in it, but she didn’t seem to notice.

“Do you have a horse?” She asked as she dismounted from hers. Once down, her gown reached the top of her shins, and the beautiful leg disappeared behind the fabric. It was disappointing, but I had more important things to do than act like a twelve-year-old apprentice at a brothel.

“No, but I do have a little for a cart if you would prefer not to walk,” I replied. I had been walking all morning, and a nice cart ride would be nice. Besides, it would help keep a cart on hand if our target also decided to ride a taxi allowing us to follow without much fuss.

“Fair enough.” She replied before turning towards her horse and dragging out two winter cloaks from her saddlebag. The coverings were wool and looked a lot like a merchant’s cloak. They were heavier and with more fabric than my own and would keep the wearer warmer. However, this would mean less movement in a fight, so it would have to do the trick of disguising us in the city’s crowds.

“I hope this will fit you. You’re pretty tall,” Jane said as she handed me mine. It was long but made for a man a head shorter. However, I figured I would make it work.

“So you think I am pretty,” I said, trying to get her to crack a smile with the play on words. It didn’t work. She looked at me with raised eyebrows before turning to Henry with a pleading stare. Henry, though found the joke humorous and had cracked a smile. It must have been evident to Jane that he liked his choice, so she shook her head and led her horse to Henry.

“I won’t be needing Splash, so make sure he is well looked after till I get back.” She said before looking back at me with one of those looks that screamed, ‘how did I end up with him.’ Then she took a deep breath and started away, calling a two-horse cart over. I had just enough time to hand Henry my usual cloak before the coach pulled up, and the coach spirited us down the lane towards the White Doe.

Knowing then what I know now, I would have enjoyed the view of the city and left Jane to herself. Through our time together, I would find that she was not one to talk very much when business was at hand. However, this truth had not dawned on me yet. Therefore I spent fifteen minutes on or ride trying to break the ice before she finally broke her monosyllabic replies.

"Do you always talk this much?" She asked. She didn't look annoyed, as her facial expressions were more curious, but it did come across a bit rude.

"Sorry, I just figured I should know the person I am working with," I said, a little agitated at her for being so withdrawn. To my surprise, she looked a little hurt by my annoyance, but she took a deep breath and spoke.

"I'm sorry," She said with sincerity as she put on the first smile I would ever see on her face. Her teeth were white and healthy, and incredibly perfectly aligned. It gave me the impression her upbringing was from a family with money. "When I am going over a mission in my mind, I generally prefer a quiet atmosphere, but I should never be so rude. What would you like to talk about?"

"You," I said in return. The truth was I like to know the skills of my companion's before going into potentially dangerous situations. Knowledge could save your life. Therefore, I started with that line of questioning. "I would love to know what you're capable of, so I know what to expect."

"That is a very fair question," She said in reply as I finally got her talking. Her body language changed to a relaxing, comfortable manner that could ease the tensest person. She looked you in the eye and spoke with clarity and smoothness that is lost often in today's world. She put a charming quality into her voice that made you want to listen. I would find out Jane liked quite most of the time. However, she was not at all afraid of socializing. Later, I would learn she was one of the most charismatic people I would ever meet when she wanted to be. "I prefer maces and my nightsticks to other weapons and am fairly good with both. My hand to hand is not bad, and I am a student of the arcane arts. I can also interrogate pretty well and speak four modern languages and ancient Amoran. I have an ally in God, but I am sure you have already guessed that and have it told to me that I have a keen mind. I do possess a few more skills, but a lady shouldn't give away all her secrets when they don't apply."

Her smile grew and became infectious as it was apparent I was impressed with her skills. My face showed it. It was true she hadn't proven any of them to me but to study in so many was rare enough. It could make her formidable if she were even halfway good at most of them.

I was also impressed by her openness and was intrigued to find out she wasn't just a Paladin. Magic was a rarity in the world, and the fact she had some mage craft was incredible. Even stranger was the fact that I had the gift as well. That gave us something in common.

Jane was now looking at me with a smile that indicated it was my turn, and I was quick to oblige. “Well, since you were so gracious, I figure I should return the favor. As you know, I am a spearman, but my main job with my previous employer was as a tracker and scout. I am not the stealthiest, but I have an excellent set of eyes and good awareness. I fight well with my hands and am not shabby with an ax. I have been trained in magic and can use several patch spells, terra, shock, and thermal.” I was hoping the magic would impress, and she did indeed seem more curious after my mention of it. Her eyebrows folded up, and she looked at me a bit sideways as if trying to decide something.

“As a scout, I would expect a sensing spell, especially if you have the symbol for thermal.” She said as she looked at me in the same way Henry had earlier. It was apparent she was his student. “So, I would be shocked if you only know the healing disciplines in bioc?”

Now I was impressed. It was apparent Jane wasn’t a novice at mage-craft. Most mages just knew spells as singular objects. Fireball, sensing touch, and earth-erode were regular spells that someone could purchase at the Mage’s Guild. Yet experienced mages could make their very own spell by rearranging the symbols.

Jane's mention of bioc as the patch spells' base form made me think she knew how to rearrange. "I do know sensing and have incorporated heat, general bioc, and magic sensing to my grouping," I said with a gloating smile. It was one of my most proud things, mostly as I had made two spells for myself. So few people had magic, and fewer took the risk to use it. It made me feel special.

"Considering our goal today, I think that skill will be the most useful." She said with a thoughtful look. "Keep it fresh in your mind, so it is ready if needed."

"If needed, I will be ready," I said as we pulled up to the building Henry had sent us.

The White Dove was not an impressive Inn. Its location was in Baker's District, which had become seedier in the past twenty years. Back then, it had housed two big bakeries. It was from them that it had gotten its name. However, those had shut down a long time ago. The area had become among the worst in the city.

The house's construction was old clay bricks that were typical for southern Broma. Yet the bricks were aging poorly, and the area looked dirty and rundown. The inn wasn't much better. It stood in the heart of the district, and as we looked at it, we noticed three rooms on the upper story that had their windows boarded shut.

“Nice place,” I said sarcastically, but Jane paid no heed. She stepped down out of the taxi and looked at the front of the building. Jane stood for a few seconds, adjusting her cloak, which was long enough to go almost to her feet. She then turned and looking at me. It was then I realized she was waiting for me to dismount. I did without haste, handed the driver his money with directions to wait till we returned. Then I followed her inside.

The inn was not nearly as bad on the inside as I had expected. The floor had a fair fresh covering of threshing, and the tables and chairs were smooth and clean. The bar’s location was on the far wall, and the stairs were on the right-hand side adjacent to it. The kitchen door was between the two as smells wafted out of the back. The aromas were surprisingly delicate, considering my preconception. However, the innkeeper was every bit as rough-looking as a mangy dog.

Jane went right up to the bar and sat down with me in tow. The barkeep eyed us for a few seconds before coming over. His greasy hands were running through a bar towel as if it, a cloth that was dirtier than the street, could magically wash away the grime.

“A bit early for you, Jane,” the keep said with a smile. His left front tooth was missing, but the smile was reasonably friendly. “Who’s your friend?”

"A business associate," she said with a surprising sweat smile back towards him. She knew the man, which surprised me. A woman of such quality was seldom known to know such a seedy-looking barkeep. Still, she did. It was just another oddity I was learning about my gorgeous companion.

"Fighter by the looks of him," He said as he looked at me up and down. This time I was annoyed at his knowledge of my profession when I was covered head to knee in a cloak meant to conceal it. "He seems capable. Who's the target?" He asked Jane as he poured her a foaming lager. My eyes looked at it with longing, but I knew better. One was never enough, so I turned my mind to something else.

"One for my companion also, Blair," She said with another smile before ignoring his other question. I promptly reordered hot tea, which got a strange look from Jane. It was fleeting but was full of curiosity as if she wondered what kind of man did not drink. She said nothing, however, and neither did the barkeep. He just sent the barmaid for my drink and then walked down the bar to wipe it down. The midday rush would be coming in soon, and he had to get ready.

"Blair has run this bar for twenty years," She said as he was out of earshot. "But I am not sure if we can trust him. Let's keep the talking to a minimum." I agreed, and the two of us sat in silence.

We waited late into the afternoon, and keeping

the silence was difficult. I was not comfortable in such a state, so I tried to keep myself entertained by reviewing my spellbook. I also had to ignore the massive amounts of liquid paradise that was just behind the bar.

Jane just sat there, fidgeting with her dark hair while occasionally glancing in my direction. It was as if she was trying to figure out my entire life with just glances.

The wait was so long that I had to keep giving the taxi driver more money to wait. During one of my returns from the taxi, I saw Blair talking to Jane, asking if she needed a refill. She had only had one the whole time, something I respected immensely, but as she refused, I saw him slip her a note. I noticed the act without giving away I had seen it, but it drew my curiosity.

Her eyes glanced at it so subtly that had I not known she had it, I would have missed the glance. Meanwhile, the barkeep started asking if we would need a room for the night. She then got up with a charming smile and said that we might be back later. She then tapped me on the shoulder and heading for the door. I was unsure what was on the paper, but I knew it was vital, so I followed her out into the street.

"He just left out the back." She said as we moved into the street. It was apparent then that Blair had either tipped her off or was leading her astray. I had thought we were keeping secrets from the man. However, it seemed they were keeping secrets from me. At that moment, I could not know what was going on, so I figured to play along till it was apparent.

“Description,” I asked as we stepped into the waiting cart?

“Just short of a quarterstaff with brown hair, grey eyes, and a grey cloak,” she never looked at me as she spoke, keeping her eyes on the road and the crowd.

“That could be half of Normandia!” I said a little bit too loudly.

“Yes, but he has a stain on the left sleeve. It was planted there last night by a skillful man and a plate of gruel.” She said as she started to look frustrated. She was looking over the crowd and couldn’t see our target. However, the hint was enough for me. Once I had it, I stood for just a few seconds, and I saw or man blending into the street at Grand and Hubert’s. I let the driver know, and he turned one block before.

“Where is he?” She asked, confused as we sped down Baker’s towards Yule’s, a street I knew would cross at Hubert’s. “I didn’t see him.”

“He is moving up Hubert’s, and I figured we could come from here and catch up to him easy enough. “My idea was sound, and as we entered Yule’s or mark could be seen strolling confidently 30 yards ahead. I motioned for the driver to slow down, and we trailed him for some time.

He stopped a few times before I realized a problem with our strategy. The cart was making us easy to spot, so I acted quickly. I got down and pretended to talk to a few vendors as we moved down the lane. I figured it would make me seem like I was shopping for my lady. It seemed to work, and or mark seemed to relax. Still, this went on for several minutes, and it became apparent he was trying to lose possible pursuit with boredom. However, Jane and I stayed fixed on our target.

The sun was waning in the sky when it happened. Our target bumped into someone so briefly that I almost missed it, but there was a paper flash. It disappeared into the new man's cloak as he walked away towards a side street. Vance had made a drop. The only question was if he let his confederates know he was actively trailed or had given them knowledge of their upcoming task. Either way, I had to know so that I couldn't let the second man getaway.

"Something just happened," I said quickly to Jane as I bolted after the new man. She was left to follow the first, and she seemed confused. She stared after me with the most agitated face before throwing her hands up and asking me something. However, the crowd was thicker than average for that time of day, and I lost her words in the noise.

I should have told her to capture Vance, but it was too late. The driver had kept moving, and the noise wouldn't allow me to tell her anything either. I just kept my eyes on the new man and followed.

We turned two more blocks before he bolted around a corner. I cursed because I could not close the distance, and I knew he had made me. I started to run and soon found myself bounding after the new mark. We went down several more blocks, but he was way faster than I was.

I lost him around the third block and was again cursing myself when I saw him reappear out of a side alley. In his haste, he had turned down an ally that had been blocked by crates. It was my luck and his cost.

I bound towards him with a powerful shoulder and was able to throw him back into the ally. The man did not speak. There was no need. He knew I was on to him, and I knew he wouldn't go without a fight. A dagger flashed out of his cloak, but my ax was already in hand.

He was a small man with quick looking feet. But it was his beady little eyes that were an awful thing about him. They seemed colder than a winter's dawn, and I knew he would kill me if he could. However, that was easier said than done.

Now I wasn't as comfortable with an ax as I was with

a spear, but I was bigger than my foe. I also had the advantage that the ally was hurting his speed, so I liked my chances.

“Give it up,” I said coolie even through my up-tempo breath. I was in good shape, and my run had been tiring but not nearly so much as his.

He didn’t say a word. Through his heavy breath, he positioned himself into a forward stance and prepared to dart at me. The foot positioning let me know he had some training, but my nerves were steel. The excitement was now throughout my core, and I knew that battle was to be our lot.

Then he struck quickly, darting forward like a viper trying to reach home. Still, I was ready. Too many years of fighting had my instincts quick as a gnome. I slid to the side and struck with the side of the ax. It hit his shoulder, bouncing off his muscles with no issue.

I cursed. I could have killed the man had I used the blade, but a dead thief couldn’t talk. However, he went to one knee from the hit, and I thought I had him. It was my mistake as he came up with a hand full of dirt. The next thing I knew, I was mostly blind. I was dodging the image in front of me through masses of tears. I blocked out the pain and concentrated hard to see my foe.

He had the advantage, but I had my braces and my

ax. The fight was hard, but I was more skilled. After a few moments more of fighting, his training started to fail. He was getting winded, and I was still fresh. More importantly, even after all his attempts, he still couldn't get around me. It was time to make my move.

It is a risk to use magic when you are tired, but I knew this spell well. I chanted quickly after repelling another short attack with my ax. Then I grabbed his slowed down wrist. It was then that my magic went off. The electricity flowed through his body, and he dropped like a sack.

I looked around for something to use to carry him and found another taxi just a block away. I jumped up and down till the driver saw me, and he then came bounding over. I put my prisoner into the back of this four-wheeled carriage, and then, after showing him my fighter's tags, I jumped in also and asked him to head back to where I had left Jane.

We went back to that location and found Jane sitting in the cart with Vance neatly tied up. She was interrogating him with a charm I had not yet seen her use. Still, Vance was good at keeping his mouth shut, and she had not learned anything.

"What did you learn?" She asked as she got out of the cart and walked over to my taxi.

"Not sure," I said as I handed her a piece of paper. "I don't speak this."

She looked at it for a few moments before declaring she didn't either. "But it is Lopsi, or I'm a troll," she stated. I sort of giggled to myself to imagine her as a troll. What one hell of a beautiful troll. However, she was already on the move, and my mind had to go back to work. I knew Lopsi was the thieves' language, but I didn't know anybody who spoke it.

However, Jane did, and in a few moments, we were back at the White Doe. She went inside to speak with Blair while I stood guard over our captives. It dawned on me that, for a man she did not trust, Jane put a lot of faith in Blair. However, we needed the information, and Jane was leading the mission. I had to trust her.

Both prisoners were awake, so in the meantime, I made every attempt to get information out of them. Yet all they would do is reply with that same strange Lopsi language. At times like those, I wished I had known mind reading, but I did not. So I was trying for a third time to get them to give me information when Jane came bolting out of the White Doe. The carriage had been housing the two prisoners, and she told the driver to take them to the first guards he found. Then we hopped in the faster cart, and off we went.

"What's going on?" I asked as I watched our prisoners get carried away.

"The plan is a distraction tactic," Jane said as she urged the driver on faster with promises of a gold piece if they got there in less than 10 minutes. "They are going to divert most of the guards and hope to draw off Henry and the Captain. Meanwhile, they are going to use two inside men to make off with the Relics. What's most important is if any of the members did not meet at the proper location, they would start the assault early, as in now!"

I didn't say a word. The plan had merit, and it would be hard to stop. Yet I remember rumors I had heard about the paladin's powers. They could sense evil, I thought, and decided to ask.

"Most of the time, they can get a general sense if evil is around," she stated as we continued to fly down different streets. Other carts and pedestrians moved out of our way, and we were making good time, "but not a direct one. However, Henry has a device for just that purpose. They must have found a way around it."

"They could be planning a two-stage attack," I said, thinking of many different scenarios where they could get around sensing of that kind, but Jane shook her head.

"Blair was adamant. The wording said that the men are with the guards, and the diversion can start as soon as everyone arrives. If not there by dusk, proceed with urgency. There are insiders." She looked adamant, and I had to admit that she had to be right. But I didn't understand her magic, so I had no idea how to get around it.

We reached the Captain's quarters where they were housing the relics, and Jane bounded out of the cart without a word. It took us only a few yards to move past the grounds' outer wall to the oddly unguarded front door. Then it became apparent why nobody was guarding it as blood was in the courtyard. Then we found two bodies stuffed just inside the door. Both had been stabbed through the neck and were dead.

The bodies were two of the four guards left to protect the relics after the diversion, and the fake guards must have already gone in. My heart was racing. My heart racing was because I was hoping we weren't too late to stop them but also because they showed they were willing to kill.

We rushed down hallways so fast that I lost track of Jane. She was faster than me, so I stopped and decided to cast a spell to look for magic. Even clerical magic would show up, but I was still surprised to see multiple magic points heading back the way we had come. I cursed and ran for it when a light came into view. It was the strangest light I ever saw as it looked like the air itself was glowing. It glowed in my sight as well as my spell and let me know it too was magic. It was surrounding Jane, who had reappeared from another room.

"They are heading for the door, stop them," she screamed as she ran with me towards the fading points of magic! My spell ran out as we ran hard and into the remaining day's light. There, in front of us, the two other guards were running away with all the speed they could. I knew I couldn't catch them, but Jane touched my arm, and the next thing I knew, I was facing or enemies and standing in their path.

They were as surprised as I was at getting ahead of them, but Jane was not. With the air around her glowing, she seemed like an angel come to earth. Yet with a steel mace in her hand and eyes as focused as stone, the only angel Jane could be was that of justice. It was an impressive looking display of power, and she followed it up with a dart of some magic web that shot from her hand. It grabbed the first man. Then she planted her feet and pulled hard. The first guard flew forward and hit face-first into the cobbles as Jane sprung forward to secure him.

The other one, however, had recovered from the shock of seeing us out in front. That guard was barreling towards Jane, so I had to act. I cast my spell again to see the guards' magic and make sure I could touch them. It allowed me to see the relics. They were in the fallen one's satchel, but the two magical helms caught my attention the most. The magic on them was so powerful that I could not read the spell they were giving off. Magic like that was troubling, but I did not have time to worry about it.

I didn't even use my ax. I tackled the running guard full around the waist putting everything into my charge. I hoped to stop him from reaching Jane. However, he was no slouch of a fighter. As I hit him, he twisted his momentum and landed on top of me. I was surprised and horrified as he now had the upper hand, but a funny thing happened. His helm was poorly fitted and went flying off in the scuffle. Therefore when he came up ready to start swinging, he suddenly stopped and shook his head like he was trying to clear it. The act made me remember the magical helms.

“The helms Jane; they are being controlled,” I said as I reached out and pushed the evil thing away from the guard and myself! He was looking at me with the most stunned eyes I ever saw. In the meantime, Jane had easily removed the other guard’s helm and had tossed it away.

“Where am I?” my guard asked as he looked around, completely unaware of the last few minutes of his life.

“Captain’s Quarters, stealing the Relics of the Sun,” Jane said as she started searching her prisoner. He looked at both of us as if we were crazy. Luckily it wasn’t more than 10 seconds later when Henry and the rest of the guards came back around the block and saw us with the two guards. They rushed forward as Jane produced the Relics out of the first guard’s pouch with a deep sigh of relief from the guard captain and a curse of surprise from the guard I had fought.

The Relics of the Sun were not that impressive looking. They were nothing more than medallions made of copper with a yellow sun painted in the middle. Still, I knew just how much trouble they could cause in the wrong hands and was thrilled we had rescued them.

“What happened?” The Captain said as he reached us first. He was an average looking guy in his mid-forties. He was salt and pepper, with blond being the original base color. He had liquid blue eyes and a grim square jaw that seemed as equally harsh as his muscular figure.

“Magic helms,” Jane said as if that was enough to explain.

The Captain quickly cast his sensing spell and let out a long whistle. “By God, those are something else. How the hell did you boys get these?”

The guard that I fought was helping me up, and he answered. “We bought them yesterday at the market. They were cheap and better than what we had.”

Joshua was about to reply when he realized there were only two guards. “And where are Dick and Robin?”

“Dead Sir,” Jane said as she pointed to the door. “They never stood a chance.”

If you have ever heard a sailor curse, it could not have been near the string of vulgarities that came out of the Captain's mouth. His face was red, and his eyes burned, but when he turned and saw Jane holding the relics, he let out another huge sigh.

"This was almost a disaster Henry." He stated as he took the relics from Jane.

"It was for Dick and Robin," Henry replied. "But it was a good thing we kept our eye on Vance."

"Indeed," The Captain said as I watched him secured the relics into his satchel. "Damn good work by your paladin Henry. Damn good work." He turned again, looking at the door. There, some other guards were looking after Dick and Robin's bodies, disgust still in his eyes.

The rest of the story sums up pretty nicely. We spent the next few minutes with the Captain and Henry as they moved the relics to another sight. They decided on the Mage's Guild after a brief walk, and soon we were sitting in the grand hall of the Normandia Tower of Arcane.

It wasn't a pure tower as most of the building was in a dome consisting of a massive three stories. But the main vault of the mage's was in its grand tower, and there they decided to let the relics stay till their use the next day. It was costly, but considering the attempt, it was worth the price. It would be unlikely anyone would have planned to steal it there since nobody had considered it as a possible location beforehand. Plus, it needed magic to reach it, so they were pretty safe.

We spent the next ten minutes, giving our story to the Captain and Henry. They listened intently to what we had to say. Then we listened to the two enchanted guards. They had only bought the helms the day before at an incredibly discounted price, but now it was apparent why such a discount. They used sensing magic to follow the two guards to the hiding place. Then, using the diversion, they could get the remaining guards under their spell and have them commit the act. It had almost worked.

Once the guards finished, Henry and Joshua let them go. It was evident that they had not done anything malicious, so there was no point in punishing them. However, they were told all new purchases must be inspected by mages before use in the future.

Then Henry and Joshua turned their attention back to me. Henry decided to pay me twice what he had promised and refunded me the money for the taxis. The Captain also threw in the same amount for my time and vowed to recommend me to the Fighter's Guild. In all, the day had turned out pretty well and could have only gone better had Jane and I had made it in time to save the guards Dick and Robin. However, the recommendation from the Captain of the Normandia guard would be a huge boost, and I couldn't help but feel that this would be the moment I needed to get my group together.

More importantly, to my future, Jane and I also spent some time talking, and I found her to be quite relaxed and open now that work was over. Her quieter nature seemed to transform into a very charismatic, friendly young lady. She was very knowledgeable about many fighting subjects and impressed me greatly with her knowledge of magic. We even toured the grounds for a few minutes before I decided it was time to leave her company.

"It was a great pleasure to have met you," I said to her as I decided to go. I was a bit sad to be ending our day's adventure as she was an amazing woman. Yet I had things that I needed to do in the morning. Plus, with the amount of magic I had cast and the running I had done, I was ready for a good night's sleep.

"The same here, Paden." She said in return as we shook hands near the great doors of the mages towers. "And I wish you luck in your venture."

"Thank you, Jane," I said in return. "It won't be easy, but I am confident I can manage."

"If you need any help, you know where to find me," she finished as she turned and started to walk away. It was an offer I would take her up on often.

"Can you request help from a Paladin at any time," I asked before she had gone very far?

She smiled and let out a laugh, “Depends, but for you, I may make an exception.”

My face turned red as I walked out the doors, and I could hear Jane’s giggle as I walked out into the street and headed back to Ozzy’s.

*Story 2*

# *The Reluctant Thief*

It had been three weeks since the adventure of the Relics of the Sun. My life was going in a positive direction. First, it allowed me the opportunity to take a couple of small cases. Both were successful and help me once more to show my reliability. Then I managed to hire two new hands. This was an exciting moment for me, and though neither was more than an amateur, it was a step in the right direction.

The first new hire was Maria Vickers. She was an attractive young woman with brown curly hair, large eyes with eyelashes that were long and lushes. She had a petite body with features that seemed to be between a girl and a woman. Her breasts and butt were small like a girl, yet she had the start of the hourglass figure, and a few more years of maturity would see her mature into a knockout.

She came from an estate of a minor lord. There she had grown up working with her parents as a servant. She was well-liked by all accounts and had even been given a good recommendation by her Lord. Her skill was in archery, and she had some promise with a bow. There were only two real weaknesses. She was terrible with hand to hand weapons and suffered from insufficient strength. It would be a test for me to get her stronger and keep her away from battle until she was ready.

My other new employee was Edward Koffing. He was a short man of the same height as Maria with light dirty blond hair that he wore long. His eyes were grey-blue, and his body was small framed. His looks were above average, but his eyes held a charm of their own that allowed him the confidence of people with little effort.

However, he did have one annoying habit. He was prejudice against peasants. His father was an ex-guild member and was very wealthy. He did not like commoners much and had taught his son the same bad habit. It was hypocrisy considering that his father had been a commoner himself, but such logic did not matter. Twice I had to reprimand him and remind him that both Maria and I were commoners, but, in his mind, fighters were above that in status. It was like talking to a wall. However, he had kept it pretty businesslike otherwise and only made comments in private, so I had little grounds to let him go. Plus, I had no other prospects at the time and needed him. Unlike Maria, he could fight up close. Even with his small size, he was capable, and I couldn't afford to lose him.

This particular day started with a training session

between my new group and me. It had been interesting, to say the least. I had spent half the day giving pointers to both of them and then testing them one on one. Unfortunately, Maria had been a pushover, and I had sent her to do some workouts while I evaluated Edward.

However, Eddie was not a disappointment. He was small, fast, and had good sword work. Eddie was well trained and aggressive. In fact, he would have been better than me except for one flaw. He was a talker.

In fact, both of them were.

There was one significant difference, and that was Maria's shyness. She didn't get talkative till she knew someone. Eddie did not share this trait. He always talked and even did it while fighting. The thing was, it caused his footwork to become sloppy. Twice already, I had put him on his back, and he was not happy.

"I don't understand how you keep doing that." He said as he picked himself off the floor. He had attacked with a good flurry, but he timed this attack in between his statements. I had no trouble timing him. Plus, his footwork was lousy. As soon as I hit him, he fell like a deck of cards. What was worse was it was not easy to get a word in to correct him.

"My father is a great fighter, and he trained me since I was old enough to hold a sword." He continued as I waited patiently for him to come to his point. "I saw a good opening and attacked quickly, yet you step to the side like you knew it was coming, and I was flat on my back again. I can't figure out how you knew I was going to attack. It's like you can read minds."

"I can yours," I said, a little annoyed. Eddie was whining and not thinking. If he took two seconds to stop talking, he could see his issue.

He looked shocked at my statement and a little hot. "Reading minds is illegal," he said with zeal! It was apparent he did not realize what I meant.

"I don't need magic to read your thoughts," I replied coolly.

"Then how do you know what I am about to do," He said, cutting me off and not letting me finish? "I keep my sword in the ready position, and I don't wind up. There is no way you can tell when I am going to attack."

He was about to continue with something, but I cut him off, "It's your talking."

He did not understand as he stopped for a second, allowing me to finish. "When you talk, you time your attacks in between statements. It messes with your breathing, kills your footwork, and I can tell exactly when you are about to strike because it is the only time you are quiet."

He looked a bit angry at the statement, but it turned out not mad at me. "You sound like my father."

"Wise man," I said in reply. He didn't look kindly at that statement.

"My father is an overbearing, hard-headed jerk." He started to say.

"And a damn good fighter," I said, cutting him off again. "He may be all those things, but the man can fight."

He looked like he was still angry, but he shook his head in agreement, hoisted his training shield, and turned to face me. He did not speak for the next match, and he did much better.

"Very good," a voice said behind us as we were still sparing! I recognized the voice and lost consideration, receiving a blow on the side of the head. It stung even through the padding, and I heard a cry of triumph and laughing at the same time. Eddie had the triumph. Jane was laughing.

"Sorry, boss," Eddie said with a bit of concern. He had struck me hard. However, I had a thick skull, and the padding meant no permanent harm.

"No problem," I said as I held my head for a few

seconds. I was not sure if it was my pain or pride that hurt more. With Jane looking on, though, I am sure now it was the pride.

She was just as beautiful as I remembered though today she was wearing a loose blouse and riding trousers. Yet even these could not make her figure look boyish. Her curvy well-formed body was spectacular, long, and hourglass just as before. It was a pleasure to behold her.

“Welcome, Jane,” I said as I took my hand off my head and shook her hand. She was still smiling, and the view was radiant.

“Good to see you too, Paden,” she half giggled. “Do you need me to heal your head?”

“Just my pride,” I answered back, but in truth, I was proud of Eddie. He had not been distracted and had taken the opening as he should.

“Well, at least you know you have good help,” she answered back. To my surprise, she talked straight at Eddie. “How’s the old man Edward?”

Eddie was also smiling to see Jane. It was a universal effect. “He is still kicking, unfortunately,” Eddie said.

“Still mad at him,” she asked? It was still a shock to

me that they knew each other. It was such a small world.

"He did kick me out of his estate," Eddie remarked back. That was not an accurate statement. He only kicked him out as long as he tried to be a fighter. Still, Eddie hadn't taken the banishment well.

"He'll get over it," Jane replied back before talking to me. "I need your help."

I could tell Eddie wanted to say something, but I had to make sure I spoke first, "what can I do for you?"

"There is a case that has come to your Guild. I need you to take it before another team takes it," she said.

"Of course," I said as I looked at her. She had become 'serious,' which was her nature, but there was urgency in her voice.

I started walking and motioned for her to follow. "Take five, Eddie and find Maria," I told him as Jane, and I walked towards the front office.

"Give me an account of the mission why we walk Jane," I asked, excited to be working with her again. I had thought about going to the Church and looking her up, but business had been in the way. I reminded myself that networking was important and promised to see more people in the future, especially Jane.

“Lord Hampton of the south Hamptons has had some house plans stolen from his estate,” she began. “He is currently starting to remold the inside of his manner, and the plans are necessary for getting the house renovated into a castle, and you know how important a castle is to the status of a lord. However, his butler Toby Grey has stolen them. The weird thing is that Toby has worked for Lord Hampton for 14 years, and no one can think of a good reason for the plans to be stolen.”

“When did this occur,” I asked as we finished our short walk to the main hall? We stopped just inside so that she could finish her story.

“Two days ago,” she replied. “It happened during the night when everyone was asleep. He apparently snuck into the main room the mason’s Guild was using as their headquarters in the manner, stole the plans, and then left. The weird part is as follows. First, the plans are not worth anything outside of Lord Hampton’s estate. Second, the locked drawer held other valuable items, and he didn’t take them, and third, he could have hidden the plans, and no one would have ever known that they were taken by him. However, his absence from the scene seems to be an admission of guilt.”

I could not argue with her. It sounded fishy, but why did she want me into this so badly? I asked her.

“I need someone I could trust,” she replied with a charming smile. I would say I must have beamed like a schoolboy because she laughed lightly at me when I heard her.

“That you can,” I said back, still smiling like a fool.

She got very serious, “You must understand I need him alive. No killing.”

Now it made more sense. Jane knew from our last adventure, I understood how to hold back. I was glad to do so.

“No issue,” I told her in reply.

She smiled and thanked me. I gave her a “you’re welcome” before I walked over to the Fighter’s Guild’s main counter and proceeded in taking the quest. Gregory, the old guild trainer, and job assigner, was behind the desk. He was pleased to give it to me without much fuss. Then I went back to Jane.

By this time, Eddie and Maria had gotten out of their sparing clothes and had come over. They were ready to go, but I was not. I excused myself, got changed, and came back in time to hear Eddie talking up a storm to the usually quiet Jane.

“You will admit that regular mage craft has its uses

over clerical," Eddie was saying to Jane. I could not believe my ears. He must realize she is a Paladin. However, Jane took it in stride.

"Of course they have the same source, so, in essence, they are similar powers," Jane answered back. I was not so sure about that but was not rude enough to argue.

"Then how is it that a mage can do good and evil and a Paladin only good," Eddie asked? It was a good question but not appropriate. I interrupted.

"Doesn't matter," I answered before Jane, "because we have work to do. You can torture Jane later."

Jane smiled, but Eddie looked annoyed. Maria, on the other hand, was being quiet. This, however, was normal when she was around someone new. It wouldn't take long before she too was talking up a storm.

"We will have to get a move on if we don't want to waste the day," I said to Jane. She agreed, but a problem arose quickly.

"I need you mounted soon then," Jane said. It then dawned on me that I would need a horse. The lucky part is that the guild rents horses. The bad part is I did not have the spare money for all three of us. I rented one for myself and left my new employees with the mission of asking around the city just in case our mark had come to Normandia. Then I went out to the stables and took the horse provided for me.

It was an older mare and probably a cross between a Mustang and a quarter-horse, but the old swayback could have been any mix in truth. She was ridden hard and shown some wear. Thus, she was lovingly called a 'slut horse' in the Guild. Everyone gets a ride, and I was glad not to be walking. Compared to Jane's Mustang, however, my rental looked sad.

"You need to get yourself a horse," Jane said as I met her out front, and we started towards our case together.

"You going to pay for it," I asked with a sly smile. Jane just laughed.

When we rode up to the estate, it was midday. The sun was out and shining, but you could feel a slight breeze, and the mid-winter cold bit deep. I was a hardy man, but I was looking forward to going inside.

It was a large estate built in a castle motif. The roof was a typical gable of the southern Broman tradition, and the mansion itself was a large L shaped building. There were six turrets on the building. Four turrets were on the corners, and two were midway from the center hall down each building branch. However, the more massive five-story castle tower on the back L's rear part was much bigger and more impressive.

The walkway was also very pleasing to the eye. It was brick cobbles that ran to a small bridge that crossed the stream at the house's front. This was made of stone and was carved with little gargoyles. These were placed much like the turrets on the corners and center of the bridge. Then the road led to a circular path that ended at the building itself. Had it been spring when the flowers bloomed, I knew this would be a breathtaking walkway.

Then there was the masonry of the building. The outside of the building was a sturdy limestone in the apple stone color. The roof contrasted this creamy beige stone with a deep grey slate. The stones fittings were smooth and even, and the stone faces were polished to a gloss. It was a lovely mixture that gave the manor finery not typical to such lesser lords. It was a reminder that we were in the affluent south, where even the lower lords had great wealth.

This was even showed at the front door. It was a massive oak door carved with ivy running up its length and beautiful ironwork to strengthen and support it. These were also in the shape of ivy, giving the door a remarkable effect.

Jane knocked using the iron door knockers. They were well placed and gave a pleasant but loud boom every time she hit. I could imagine that anybody in the building could hear them regardless of where they were inside the building. They also gave us or desired effect as soon a middle-aged man opened the doors.

"Good afternoon," The man said with grace. He was of average height with a slim build, dark hair, and a hooked nose. He was dressed in a lovely tunic and good linen slacks while his shoes were nice black leather. "How can I help you today?"

Considering that I was dressed in my brass chest plate and Jane had on her mail, I thought it a silly question, but proper protocol had to be kept. "I have an appointment with Lord Hampton, and my friend here is the leader of a fighter's guild group that has taken up his request," Jane said in reply.

"You are expected," He returned as he motioned us in. The inside of the estate was not nearly in the same condition as the outside. The floors were oak but showed signs of old water damage. The inside stone was a beer stone and rougher in texture than the outside's beautiful fascia. Even the tapestries looked old and worn. It was apparent why the master of the house was remodeling. It just seemed he started from the outside in.

Our greeter showed us to a waiting room with a lovely warm fire. He then pulled out a bottle of brandy and two glasses before leaving us so he could get his master. The brandy looked tremendous, but I declined as usual. This brought a smile to Jane's lips, who had seen this behavior in me before, and I smiled back. However, neither of us spoke till Lord Hampton came in.

He was a stately looking man who held himself with shoulders back and head held high. However, his walk was anything but stiff. He had a fluid grace about him that seemed to make him appear younger than his salt and pepper hair. He was also still a stout, well-muscled man and looked formidable despite his age. However, the guard with him was armored and armed, making any of the Lord's skills unnecessary.

The guard stayed near the door while he approached us at the table. We went to stand up, but he waved us to remain seated. He then pulled up a chair himself, poured each of us some more of his brandy, and then began to speak.

"I am pleased you came so promptly," he began with a sip of his brandy as a pause. He looked like a man who was used to things running smoothly and was highly annoyed at the inconvenience. I was not sure what made me feel that way until I saw the tightness in his mouth as he spoke. "The incident occurred two days ago, and I have had no ends of trouble getting the Mason's Guild to continue the work without the plans. They are worried about the wall structure and are spending more time drawing new plans for the house and slowing down their work."

"That is essential, Lord Hampton, or you may have a collapse of your structure," I replied. I do not know why I was defending the Mason's Guild, but old habits die hard.

“I understand the dangers,” Lord Hampton bit back, “but the new pace is costing me financially on an already expensive build.”

“My apologies, sir,” I replied angrily to myself for getting him more upset. I knew better and didn’t want him to lose trust in me.

“It is no issue,” he said back. “My anger is with Mr. Grey for putting me in this situation, and I am hopeful you can resolve this quickly.” Then he changed his attention. Up to this point, he had been talking to me, which I had failed to recognize. Now he was looking at Jane.

“As for your involvement, my lady,” he stated, “I continue with my objection. I will not deny the Church, but taking up this case in such a fashion when guilt is already obvious seems a waste of your time and mine.”

I was confused, but Jane answered back. “A man’s guilt is sometimes more hidden than we assume my Lord and my leaders feel this warrants our involvement. Even if my presence is for no more than judgment, I am obliged to be here.” All this was over my head.

“Do they assume I would judge unfairly?” This the Lord said with a bit of venom.

"It is unsure, sir, where the issue may lie," she responded, "but my orders come from a greater power, and HIS call warrants my investigation." She was speaking of God, of course, and Lord Hampton did not respond. There was no need. Such a call trumped everything though he made no attempt to hide his disgust.

Jane then spoke up, "to do that, we may need some information. What can you tell us about the night the plans were taken?"

Lord Hampton took a deep breath. Obviously, he didn't like the situation as it stood, but he had no choice but to accept her involvement. "I will do what I can and have already given my entire staff the order that they are to assist you to the best of their ability." He made sure he looked at both of us when he made that statement.

"That is helpful," She replied in return. "So, what can you tell us about that night?"

"There is not much to tell," He began. "The night was not much different than any other. After I was finished with my day, and the Masons had retired to their quarters, I took the estate plans to my workroom. Then I locked them into my desk before retiring for the evening into the inner chamber. The next morning I found my desk unlocked and the plans gone. I called for Mr. Grey as he is the only one other than me with a key, but he was not in the castle. I asked my night guard where he was, and he said he saw him leave in the night. He also said he saw him carrying the plans with him as he left. However, as my main butler for 14 years, he figured there was a good reason for it and let him leave. I have since fired the guard."

"Then there is no doubt he took them," Jane said, sounding a bit disappointed.

"No doubt at all," Lord Hampton replied, making sure she understood this was a fact.

"How much are the plans worth," Jane then asked, going down the next obvious line of questions?

"Priceless to me if I ever want this old house to stay in one piece," the Lord said in return.

"But to anybody outside of this estate, they are useless," I answered. I had been a mason. I knew plans.

"Not useless," said the guard who was standing near the door. I recognized he was a guild member as I had seen him in the Guild a few days before. However, he was referred to as a 'root' because he had been hired by a client permanently. It was an excellent way to get quality warriors. As for the guards, it was a great gig and safer than adventuring. It was where many of the grunts went when they retired. "Lord Hampton has some wealth between the horse ranch and other ventures. A thief may find it useful."

It did not make sense to me. "But if the butler wanted to steal, he could have just let the thieves in," I said.

"Not with my night guard," Lord Hampton answered back. "I keep him stationed to make sure nobody gets in who is not supposed to be here. Even if my last guard let the plans out, I guarantee that even he would not be so stupid as to let a stranger in."

"Then the plans are to allow someone to get around your guard," Jane said. "Has there been any weakening of the outside walls or a tunnel made during the renovations?"

"None," Lord Hampton said, sounding a little frustrated with the direction of the conversation. It was apparent the idea of what Toby Grey was possibly up to disturbed the Lord. "Do you think he could have gotten his wife to stay behind to draw the guards off?"

It sounded like a possible idea, but Jane was quick to point this out as illogical. "No," she said in a reassuring tone. "It would make no sense to leave someone behind for the same reason Mr. Grey didn't stay behind. Lord Hampton, you already said that they couldn't get past the guards, and now your men are suspicious about a possible break-in. It only makes sense that they are looking for a way around the guard with the plans."

"But there is only the front door," Lord Hampton insisted. "If they want in, they would have to go that route, and my guard is stationed there. Stealing the map was a dumb thing for Mr. Grey to do, and now he will pay with the stocks."

I had to agree with the Lord while Jane seemed to be mulling everything over in her mind. I found it an excellent time to ask a few questions myself.

"So Lord Hampton," I started. "Is Mr. Grey an outdoorsman?" I really was not interested in the reasoning behind the theft, regardless of how interesting. I only wanted to know where to find Mr. Grey, and I figured I could narrow it down to a few short questions.

However, it must have seemed an odd question to the rest of the group because they all looked at me as if it was something strange to ask.

"I need to know if I should be checking for him in the woods or in the city," I explained. "If he is an outdoorsman, he may feel more comfortable outside of the city."

"Man couldn't string a...," The guard was probably going to say bow, but Mr. Hampton cut him off.

"Mr. Jake," He started, annoyed. "You are a guard, not an advisor. Stand there and do your job. Let me do mine."

I was stunned at the harsh treatment, but Jane and the guards seemed little affected. For my part, I tried to pass it off as if I had not seen it.

"He was terrible in the outdoors fighter," the Lord said with authority. "He is not even good with the horses and has burnt himself starting fires in a fireplace. Outside of the comforts of civilization, he would not last long."

It was the first of the things I felt I needed. If Mr. Gray was useless outside of a city, he would have to go to one, and once in civilization, he would need help. "Does he have family or friends in the city," I followed up?

The Lord was smiling at the line of questioning. I was obviously looking for what he wanted, the culprit. "I know he has someone in Normandia, but I never delved too deeply," the Lord said. "His wife will know, however."

I nodded my head in agreement. I had a direction to work towards and felt comfortable Mr. Grey's wife would lead me to his in-city relative.

"Did Mr. Grey have access to everything in the manner," Jane asked? I realized she had been sitting there not listening to us for the last few moments but was deep in thought. “Could he get into the vault without you?”

“Yes,” Lord Hampton simply answered, annoyed at the return to that line of questioning. “Why?”

“We assumed he stole the plans for money purposes, but if he was going to do that, why not just steal the money,” she said in reply. “But for the life of me, I can’t think of another reason to take the plans but to try to rob the coffers.”

“Madam Paladin...,” Lord Hampton started before a knock came to the door, and the new butler came in.

“Your brother...,” he started to say, but Lord Hampton was furious.

“How dare you interrupt my meeting,” Lord Hampton basically screamed at the butler. “My brother can wait till this is over. Send him to the study!”

The butler seemed indifferent to being yelled at, but Jane and I wore our shock. Luckily we both mastered ourselves before he looked back at us. Jane quickly sipped her drink while I pretended to study the butler.

The butler left under the heated stare of Lord Hampton before it was our time to receive his view.

“That brother of mine always arrives at the worst times,” Lord Hampton said with anger. “If he can’t keep his own affairs in order, he should spend less time messing with mine.” He then poured himself another shot and drained it in one gulp.

“Is there anything else you need,” He asked as he was obviously now both angry and agitated?

“What is the story of your brother,” Jane asked. It was a good question but harmed Lord Hampton’s mood.

“My family affairs our mine Paladin,” he said with enough heat to let everyone in the room know he meant to keep them to himself. “I have not asked you about yours, and since it has no bearing on your mission, you will look no further into mine.”

I saw her eyes shoot up, and I thought she was about to let him have it, but again she mastered herself. She simply replied, “My apologies, my calling often leads me down private lanes. I simply was here in the Church’s service and often have to ask troubling questions.”

“I prefer you focus on Mr. Grey,” Lord Hampton said with just a little more bite after Jane’s smooth reply. “So, since there is nothing else, I have some business to attend to. Mr. Perkins will be back in a moment and will take you wherever you need to go on the grounds.”

We thank him as he got up from his chair and left with the guard. When he had left, I let out a breath I did not know I was holding.

“I wouldn’t blame the brother for being trouble with a man with that temper,” I said with a smile when he had left the room. Jane, however, was lost in thought. She had her hands folded together, her arms resting on the armrests, and her head resting on her thumbs. She was deep in thought.

I was just starting to think she hadn’t heard me when she broke the silence. “Lord Hampton is under stress,” she began. “It is unfair to make a snap judgment at such a time.”

“What are you thinking about,” I asked, feeling she had heard something that had her thinking? She didn’t get the time to reply. Mr. Perkins walked in right then and asked us where we wanted to go. It was too easy a question, and soon we were sitting in front of Mrs. Grey.

“Please, Mrs. Grey,” Jane started when we got comfortable in the Grey’s large suite in the East Wing. It was a nice room with enough space for two dressers, a closet, a rarity in Broma, and a queen-sized bed. There were also two lounge chairs near a fireplace and a window that actually had a glass pain. It was wealthy surroundings for servants. “Can you tell us about your husband?”

Mrs. Grey was sitting on the bed, and Jane and I had pulled up the two chairs to talk to her. She was a middle-aged woman of poor beauty. She was plump with small eyes, a big nose, and thin lips. Her hair was salt and pepper, and her wrinkles were already a dominant feature of her face. However, there was a kindness about the lady that made her endearing just by a look.

The situation had obviously taken its toll on her as red eyes, and wet cheeks indicated her sorrow. "What do you need to know," she asked in a weak voice?

"Tell us if your husband was doing anything strange the last few days," Jane specified.

She seemed hesitant, and I figured that she was not going to cooperate. However, Jane started glowing softly, filling the room with a soft light. I had seen her do this before during our first adventure, but this time there was a soothing effect. It instantly affected Mrs. Grey.

"He had been acting odd for a few days," she began. "The first thing I noticed was that he was nervous about something. He had not been sleeping well and tossed all night long." She took a deep breath. Talking about this obviously hurt her and made her relive the strange dance of regret and relief. "I tried to ask him the matter, but he would just tell me he was worried about his mother. Three days ago, the day before he...," she stopped with a sob but after a few seconds returned to talking. "Before the incident, I saw him looking over a note with anger and threw it into the fireplace. I didn't get to see what it said, but I did get this."

She handed us a piece of paper. It was written in bold script, and I supposed it was a man's writing. 'I understand your issue Toby and feel deeply for your troubles, but this is a matter I can't help you with.' It was signed 'Arden.'

"Arden is one of Toby's boxing mates," Mrs. Grey said as she saw us reading.

"He's a fighter," I said, surprised!

"My husband fights at the Red Dragon," she answered back with pride. "He is 15 and 4."

That was a good record, but my biggest surprise was the fact he was a fighter. The Guild was not the only place where fighters went to box, but it was rare that they were not involved. If they were, then Mr. Grey was a member.

"Is he a guild member," I asked, needing to know if the Guild had information. They kept good records, and they could be valuable.

"No," she replied to my dismay. "The Red Dragon's

fights are in-house only. They don't include Fighter's Guild because the Guild would want their proceeds from the fighters and the event. We live well but don't have a lot of money. Toby didn't want to have to give his winnings to the Guild."

"So there is gambling," I stated. It was an obvious statement, but Mrs. Grey was quick to defend her husband.

"My husband doesn't gamble there, just fight," she stated. "We have plenty here and are not in need. He is a good man and wouldn't risk us by gambling." She was looking at Jane as if pleading with her to help defend Toby.

Her very insistence on his lack of gambling made me feel confident he was. It made no sense that he would partake in a sport that was about little else and not get involved. If he owed debts, he might have to pay them off, and stealing was one way to do it.

I turned to Jane, who seemed to be in thought still in the same manner I had seen her earlier. I had never seen her thinking deeply until that day, but I would learn it was her normal position when doing so. I then decided to ask the most critical question I had left.

"Where does your Mother-in-Law live?" I asked.

She looked a bit startled. "Please don't tell her," she

begged. I was surprised, but she was very animated about this one point. “She is an old lady with a weak heart. The shock would kill her, and I couldn’t bear to see her pass. She has been so good to me.”

I looked towards Jane, who had come out of her thought. “She already knows about the whole affair,” Jane said with a gentle smile. “She is the one who asked me for help.”

This brought a look of hope on Mrs. Grey’s face, but it had confirmed my suspicion. I had initially assumed that Jane was working for Sir Hampton, but or interview with him made it clear she was not. Now her real employer was reviled, and it would mean her sympathies were with Mr. Grey and not the victim. I did not know what she was playing at, but I was undoubtedly curious and a little upset that she was keeping things from me.

“Do you think you can save him,” Mrs. Grey asked?

“There is hope,” she said. I was now getting angry. In hindsight, I must admit that there was hope, but at the time, I couldn’t see a way out for Toby Grey. I thought getting the lady’s hope up was a bad idea.

At this, Jane stood up and left the room with me following right behind her.

“You mean to tell me that you already knew about the

mother," I said as we were halfway down the hall. I was a little hot because she left me in the dark, but I kept my voice low.

"I didn't want to bias you," she replied back, sounding a bit hurt. I was upset. "I could be wrong, and I don't want my bias filtering to you."

"But you are leaving me in the dark on information," I said with a bit a venom. I took a deep breath. "I want to help you find this guy, but I need to know your thoughts."

"I can't," she said sternly.

"Why not," I asked a little too loudly?

She became a bit stern when she replied. "Paden, you must trust me. I have my reasons."

"I like you, Jane, but I don't know you that well," I said back. I should have bit my tongue.

The look on her face spoke volumes. I had hurt her, and she could not mask it fast enough to keep it from showing. "Well, I trust you," she said back as she walked away down the hall towards Mr. Perkins, who was waiting for us. I was now both pissed and ashamed. I felt I was right, but I handled it wrong and now wanted to kick myself.

We spent the rest of the time in the manor speaking little to each other. However, we did manage to get through interviewing the rest of the staff without issues. I learned that Sir Hampton had a temper to match his outbursts during our interview, but shockingly every one of his employees loved him. His personality was fiery, but his actions spoke of a different kind of man. He was the type of employer who would yell at you all day long and then give you a bonus for an excellent job done, and though his temper was not endearing, his gifts of money and time off were.

We also learned that he was a widower who had lost two children, one to fever and one during childbirth. It was during that same childbirth that his wife had died. His only family left was his brother. The situation had left Lord Hampton as a bit of a hermit. He rarely left the house. He only left to go around the farm, watching the horses and going over his new project down at the river.

This was a side mystery that had me thinking. Sir Hampton went down to the river every day and had made plans to build something out there. However, nobody in the house knew what. I would have asked Lord Hampton, but he had gone to the river tonight, and again Jane seemed to divert my questioning. She knew what it was, it was apparent, but she was not going to tell me. Even though I wanted to press her for the information, the uncomfortable feeling we were currently feeling kept me quiet.

We left the manner, and Jane said goodbye. She was short with it but did give me the message that she was working her lead and would check back at the manor in the afternoon the next day. I agreed to the meeting and left for the city.

It was very dark by the time I got back, and my rental horse was tuckered out. I got the horse to the Guild and gave her to the hand with an extra silver to make sure the old thing had some oats for the night. I then went in search of Eddie and Maria.

Eddie had left no message, but Maria was in the Guild. I found her training in the back, working on her strength. This was another disappointment for me. I had expected both of my new employees to be working together, not splitting up as soon as I turned my back.

“Where's Eddie,” I asked? I was too tired to get angry; it had been a long day. However, her answer was enough to get me mad for the second time in the day.

“I don't know,” she said shyly. I kept my cool, but that was unacceptable.

“And the mission,” I asked next? She could see I was not happy.

“I went with him to a few bars around town,” she said. “But after the third one, he got mad at me. He said I was too clingy and not working the crowd, so he sent me back here saying he could work better by himself."

"I told you to work together," I answered. "Why did you let him send you back?"

"I..," she started, but I cut her off.

"It doesn't matter now," I said. Getting angry at Maria today would do no good. It would be best to talk to the two of them later when work wasn't needed.

"We will find him later. Right now, we need to go to the Red Dragon. Get your town gear." I ordered her. She was looking a little like she was getting ready to cry, but I did nothing. I was still in a dark mood from the way I had left Jane and, in hindsight, was taking it out on Maria. Still, leaving a partner without backup was not good practice with such inexperienced members. I would have to hammer home some better discipline.

Maria was soon ready, and the two of us made our way to the Red Dragon. We arrived to find it was a nondescript old building in the beer district. The name of the community was because of the type of stone used in the construction. With years of rain and grime, the buildings looked dingy. However, once inside, the care of the district was much better than other parts of town. The floor was stone and was well swept, the chairs were of higher quality, and the crowd seemed to be well dressed and primarily merchant class.

Compared to the White Doe, this bar was in great shape.

In the center of the room, there was a circle drawn on the floor. It was the fighting circle and was currently in use. If mainly because of being overweight, two considerable sized men were slugging away at each other with soft mitts on their hands. I laughed at myself. Fighting with mitts would never catch on, but that was amateurs for you.

I walked up to the bar with Maria in tow and sat down at the bar. The bartender was an older lady with wrinkled skin but lively eyes and a warm smile. "What can I get you, honey," she asked me.

"I need to speak to the owner," I answered and showed her my fighter's tags.

"He doesn't allow guild members," she said as she started to walk away. I caught her by the wrist. She looked at me like I must be joking, but she didn't call the bouncer.

"It's not about the fighting," I told her, flashing the badge again. "One of the owner's fighters may be in trouble."

She drew her hand away with a jerk before walking over to a large man. I figured he was the bouncer, but I was not worried. If need be, I could handle myself.

However, the man turned out to be the owner.

“You’re here about Toby,” he asked with a sneer?

“I am trying to help him,” I lied, hoping his friend would fall for it. He didn’t.

“And I am a greased pig.” He actually did look like a greased pig, but I wasn’t going to tell him that. “As for you, I have nothing to say. I already told the little rat earlier that we don’t know where he is.”

“Too bad,” I said with a smile. “I know Captain Joshua on a personal level. He won’t be happy if I have to ask him to get the information.” The truth was I knew the Captain but was not even sure if his name was actually Joshua. This bluff worked, though. The bar owner turned a few different colors before settling down and sitting next to me. I figured all the betting was not above board.

“I really don’t know where he is, but some of the boys are moving his mother out of her house tonight.” He said in earnest. “We can keep this quiet?”

“Why are they moving his mother?” I asked. This was curious behavior. Then a thought occurred to me before the owner even answered. “That’s why Jane is working for her.”

Both the owner and Maria were looking at me like I was insane. However, I now understood that time was critical.

“Do you know where that small man was that came in earlier?” I asked. I needed Eddie and wanted to curse him for not keeping the Guild informed of his progress.

“I don’t know.” The owner said, looking scared at the excitement he saw in me. “He left shortly after he came in.”

That was not helpful, but if Eddy was worth my hiring him, he did not leave empty-handed. “Did anybody else leave right before him that may know about Toby’s mother?”

The owner thought about it for a second and then cursed. “Jay did! You think that little weasel followed him.” The owner didn’t look pleased.

“I hope so,” I answered back, quickly moving on to my last question. “Where does Toby’s mother live?”

The answer was not a surprise. It was in Gold District, a small section of town that was once high-end inns and brothels. Now it was low rent apartments consisting of one or two rooms in former inns or small duplexes that had housed the better hookers. That sort of prestige had long since moved on, and now only the poor's dingy life made their lives there.

I thanked the barkeep, and with Maria in tow, we took a cab to the directions he gave us. Maria was unusually quiet. Whether Maria was shying away from my displeasure or surprised at my sudden and mysterious understanding of the situation, I didn't know nor care. My mind was running, and I was impatient to get to the heart of the problem.

We arrived at our destination a few minutes later. It was a rather large duplex on Ave D that looked a bit well kept for that part of the town. It was freshly painted, had some nice small garden boxes in the windows, and looked to have had new patching on the roof. It was still an old building, but it looked passable. It was also very active as two large burly men were busy stuffing things into a wagon while an old lady looked on. I could also see Eddie standing a block over pretending to lounge outside a small barbershop. I went there first.

Eddie didn't look that surprised to see me. In fact, he had barely acknowledged my presence before starting to talk. "I figured you would end up here," he began as I walked up to him, "I was hoping to have you here when they started off towards Toby."

My first reaction was to berate him for not letting me know where he was, but time was not on our side. "We can't wait till then," I said as I scanned the crowd. I couldn't see the other men I expected, but

I expected Toby's friends were being watched. "If we follow this group, they will lead the others strait towards Mr. Grey, and I suspect he won't live the night." Both of them were now staring at me like I had turned into a pink and purple spotted eel, but I ignored them. "We have got to get them to lead us to Mr. Grey before that can happen. Come with me."

I didn't stop to look to see if they were following. I walked coolly and confidently up the street and right towards the two men and Mr. Gray's mother. They, of course, saw me coming in my shining if not ancient, breastplate. One of them quickly led Mrs. Gray into the house while the other pulled out a long dagger and faced me. I didn't hesitate.

I pulled out my fighter's tags and held up my other hand while stopping some distance away. My only quick movement was to stop Eddie from pulling his sword.

"That's Mr. Grey's friend," he said quietly.

I felt relieved. That meant that the other man was also his friend. However, I needed to get the man disarmed so we could talk.

"Jay, I don't want a fight," I said with a calm but authoritative tone. "You know why I am here."

"You just need to turn around, Fighter." He stated

back as he brandished the knife. He was nervous, but he held the blade like a man who had handled one before. It was his footing that had me at ease. He leaned on his back foot, a naturally passive stance that gave the impression he wanted to flee. He was scared, and I could use it either for talking or fighting.

“I know why Toby did all this,” I said. I expected him to try to find out what I really knew, and I wasn’t disappointed.

“And what is it you think you know,” He asked without letting his guard down.

“Toby’s mother was threatened for the plans,” I said as I now was holding both hands up, showing as much calm body language as I could. “He should know that the thugs won’t stop till they tie up loose ends. Let me help.”

I was sincere. It was the only thing that made any sense, but Jay was still nervous. “How do I know you aren’t one of them?”

It was a valid question, but it was easy enough to solve. “I can bring a priest from the Church here. They can verify that I am a friend of the Paladin Jane.”

That was enough for the old lady. Without hesitation, she stepped back out of her house and told Jay to put down the knife. She had obviously been a lady of leisure in her more attractive youth. She had a small tattoo on her wrists that the hookers used to identify themselves, and though her beauty had faded, she still wore the yellow clothing to match her old profession.

“I believe you.” She said with confidence. Jay was not easily persuaded, but when I approached and sat on the back of the wagon with no sign of aggression, he relaxed. I then sent Eddie and Maria to watch the street while Jay and the old Lady came up and stood near me.

“I had heard of his problems at the castle the day they happened,” she started. “I have a friend in the market who sells to their cook. They got a message to me the same day, and I went straight to Jane. I knew she would help, for I knew my son was not that kind of man.”

I nodded in agreement and urged her to continue. “Toby hadn’t talked to me, but I next sent a message to the Red Dragon asking for help there. They are the ones who let me know he was giving the plans away to keep me safe. I begged them to stop him. I am old, and my life isn’t important, but my son had already made the drop. The bastards had then tried to kill him, and he barely got away with his life. He then sent his friends to collect me and get me out of the city. Once I was safe, he was going to go to the guard and tell everything.”

I listened to her why she talked and knew the problem now was to get to him safely. I couldn't do that till she was safe.

"Moving your stuff won't help, madam," I said as I thought of a plan. "You are the only thing of importance, and I know just where to house you while we get your son to safety. I will have my group and Jay's buddy here take you to the Church. In the meantime, I will go to Toby and get him safely to Lord Hamilton's Estate. From there, we can move on to the next problem of finding the thugs. "

The plan seemed to have merit, but Jay was still a problem. "I still don't trust you," he said. I had to admire his resiliency and bravery but time was short.

"You don't have a choice." I simply said. I thought for a second, he would do something foolish, but a gentle hand on his shoulder was enough to stop him.

"I have lived here my whole life Jay," Toby's mother said softly. "My stuff and my son are all that I have left, but I would give up every last item and my life for my son, and right now, this fighter is our best choice. If he is an imposter, then so be it. My death would allow my son to go to the guard. If he isn't, then he is our best hope. Let him do his job."

I was amazingly clear logic and did the job. Jay stood down, and within minutes we were traveling to the Church. I noticed two men following us after we left and made a mental note to myself, but I figured they were after Toby first, so Mrs. Jackson should be safe. They knew her death would only loosen his tongue. He had to be the first mark.

We reached the Church and left Mrs. Jackson with a priest named Sebastian, Jay's partner, and Maria. After that, Eddie, Jay, and I left for Toby. Jay wouldn't say where we were going, but it didn't matter. My first problem was our tail.

As we filtered through town, I reached a spot I knew well near my old boss Ozzie's house. I had the cab pull around quickly, jumped off behind a building, and waited. It didn't take long. A second cab turned the corner, and I recognized it was the men following us. I almost missed jumping aboard but managed the handhold at the rear of the cab and pulled myself up.

By this point, my cab had stopped, and Eddie and Jay were getting out weapons drawn. I had warned them what I was about to do, and they were ready. The men in the cab were not.

They pulled up quickly as our cab had the road blocked. The two men tried to get out, but I had one by the collar and to the ground before he could react. Jay had his villain down quickly too, but with the present. A small gash on the four-arm was Jay's reward. However, it was a minor scratch and was worth it for the protection we were providing his friend.

The second cabbie thought this was a robbery and took off running past me screaming for guards, but I called Eddie to stand ready with his tags and explanation when they arrived. In the meantime, I asked my captive the only question I needed to know.

“Who’s hired you,” I asked?

I thought he would pee himself. He was a big man with a receding hairline and massive arms. His knuckles were callused, and his jaw looked hard, but he saw the ax in my hand. This left him shaking under my grip.

“Steven,” he swore, his breath coming quickly. “That is all I could get from him. He hired us at the Red Rose, where we bounced. It was good money.”

“Didn’t it ever occur to you that this would be criminal? You had to know you would be chased by guards are fighter’s Guild,” I said more than asked. His face told me he didn’t think that far. It was disgusting, and I wanted to split his skull just for the emptiness of it. Stupidity should be a sin. But he was no longer a threat.

The guards came a few moments later, and they quickly dragged the men off. They also offered us help but could tell us nothing more about any Steven’s they knew. So with nothing else to do, we once again headed for Toby.

We reached a familiar Inn in Baker's district. I couldn't believe it when we arrived, but here was the same inn I had gone to with Jane during the Relics case. The same old barkeep was there and the same nasty toothless grin.

He acknowledged my presence, but we didn't talk. We followed Jay up the stairs and turned a corner down the left-hand hallway. It was the last door on the right that we stopped at.

"Toby, it's me, Jay." I heard a few footsteps, and Toby opened the door wide. It was foolish. Had Jay been captured, it could have been a trap, but Toby was a butler, not a spy. He looked surprised at me as I walked past him and then curiously at Jay.

"Who is he," he asked as he looked ready to run out the door? It was then he noticed Eddie blocking it.

"He is from the fighter's guild," Jay said as he put his hand on Toby's broad shoulders in greeting. "He is here to help."

"But if the fighter's guild gets involved, they will kill my mother," He said with understandable fear.

"Your mother is safe at the church under guard." I said back, "but I need to know everything from the beginning to help you."

He looked surprised, but he had no choice. He was not a stupid man. He had been dealing with Lord Hampton's Estate for years, and nobody got to that kind of trust by being stupid. He knew the only course left to him was talking.

"He first approached me at the pub after one of my fights," he began. "He bought me a few drinks, chummed around with me a few times, and even scouted a potential fight for me. I thought he was friendly enough, and during one of our conversations when I had drunken a little too much beer, I let him know just how much access I have." He stopped for a second catching himself, "had at Lord Hampton's."

"It was the next fight on my way home that he got me. He told me he needed a way into the building. He wouldn't tell me why. When I refused, he started describing my mother, her house, and her furniture. I knew a threat when I heard one. The obvious choice was to let him in after distracting the night guard. It would have been easy enough, but I couldn't betray Lord Hampton after all he has done for me, so I told him I could get him the plans of the house that would show him a way in."

"My hope was to stall long enough to get him caught, but there came a note two days ago that made it clear he couldn't wait any longer." I saw him shiver at what the note said. "I also got a note from my fighting boss saying he couldn't help. I saw no choice, so I stole the plans and headed to the meeting place. I knew the plans would be of little use for an assassin. There is no way in but the front door or the rear tower door, but one is locked and protected by a steel grate. The other is guarded. He could never get in. I think he realized this because I was only a few blocks away when his thugs tried to kill me. They had knives."

The rest of the story was pretty much as I expected. Toby fought off the two thugs we caught, ran for this inn, and sent Jay a message. Jay then acted, trying to get his mother out of the city. However, his mother had already contacted the Church.

"Lord Hampton may still be in danger," I stated bluntly when he finished. Two guards had already arrived by this time and had heard most of the story. Toby looked defeated, and Jay restless, but I had no fears.

"I need this man to come with me to Lord Hampton's estate. He needs to tell his story directly to the Lord." I got no arguments from the Guards. Soon I found myself in another cab paid for this time by Toby and riding quickly out to Lord Hampton's estate.

We arrived in the middle of the night, and the four of us got out. I had barely knocked on the door before it was thrown wholly open, and Mr. Perkin's was standing there in his nightshirt. He was awestruck at seeing Toby but did not leave us out in the cold.

"Mr. Fighter's guild sir," he began forgetting my name in the excitement and hour. "You found Toby!"

“That he has,” said a voice from behind. It was the Lord himself also in his nightshirt but with two guards with him fully armed, “but oddly not restrained.”

“Once you understand what is going on you will understand why. Eddie, guard the door with Mr. Perkins.” Both Eddie and Mr. Perkins looked a little taken aback, but I moved to the waiting room we had used that afternoon and took the group with us.

Lord Hampton didn’t hesitate. He followed directly behind us and had the door shut as soon as we entered. He then sat in his seat and simply stated, “Well?”

I prompted Toby, and he told the full story. Lord Hampton sat listening. He gave away no emotion or inkling of what he was feeling until the end of the story. Then when Toby finished, he turned to one of his guards.

“Confine Mr. Gray to his quarters with his wife till I decide what to do. Then I want both of you to return to me. We must plan.” Lord Hampton had hardly spoken before the guards took Toby and Jay away up towards his usual room. I still had to give Jay credit for his loyalty.

Once we were alone, lord Hampton turned towards me. “I must admit I am pleased that you were the one to capture him even if the Paladin ladies ideas may have some merit. Still, I am not sure how much to believe." I would have tried my best to convince him, but a knock came at the door just at that time. Then Mr. Perkin's voice rang through the door.

"My Lord, the Paladin Lady has arrived for an audience."

We both looked at each other, a bit shocked as neither of us heard a knock at the front door, but when we opened up the study, Jane was standing there.

"I will never get used to you Priests showing up just when the conversation turns to you. I swear your ears are larger than a hound's," he smiled, but Jane was in work mode and kept her smile small.

"I have news for you," she said as she looked at me as if trying to figure out what I knew. "I know Toby has arrived and I also assumed he has told you a story about an assassin?"

"That he has my lady," Lord Hampton answered back, "your doing?"

I was much more furious at the Lord for that comment than Jane was. She took it in stride and simply smiled. He was still trying to prove her wrong for some reason, and the disrespect was ungentlemanly.

She walked past him with grace and laid a hand on my shoulder. I had not realized how tense I was, but her mere touch was enough to calm me.

“I won’t have to wait long. Our assassin is just outside as we speak and will shortly enter the castle. He merely waits for the fighter’s Guild to leave. That is why I snuck in.”

“How did you get into the house with both entrances locked?” Lord Hampton asked, stunned.

“The same way he will. He will teleport,” she answered.

I almost kicked myself, but Lord Hampton made the sign of light and said a small prayer. It had never occurred to any of us that someone would use such an entrance.

“But doesn’t someone have to see a spot to teleport,” I asked? I knew little about clerical magic, but I had heard that much.

“No,” she answered. “But if they jump blindly they could end up inside a wall or in the middle of a piece of furniture. That would be death.”

“Thus the map,” Lord Hampton said with a sneer. “Then Mr. Gray led him to me.”

"He too didn't think of that kind of entrance," Jane said as she looked Lord Hampton in the eye. "But his taking of the plans did serve his other purpose. It brought help in time. Now, all we need to do is make the assassin think that the cost is clear and he will walk right in."

I saw where this was going, but it was dangerous for Jane. "I would have to leave then."

"Yes Paden," she replied with a sad smile. As usual, I could not help but smile back.

"And when he leaves the assassin will think it is just me and my two guards and attack," Lord Hampton said with the most sinister grin I had seen on a man in years. "I am starting to like the way you think Paladin."

The plan was set, and I was destined to leave. I gathered Jay and Eddie, and we started for the door. I told no one else of the plans and made it seem to Eddie that the mission was over. However, Jane gave me a note addressed to guard Captain Joshua and told me to deliver it as soon as I arrived. Then we left for the long ride home.

That cab ride was miserable. I wanted to know how it turned out, and I could not fain patients. I was exhausted by that time, but I still could not sleep. My thoughts were of Jane and the assassin. If she got hurt when I was not there, I could not forgive myself for leaving.

We arrived at the city, and I took the letter straight to the guard captain. He took one look at it and was off like a shot. He gathered six good men, thanked me, and without explanation, rode off. Eddie and I then said goodbye to Jay, went to the Church, picked up Marie, and then went to the Guild for rest. Despite my anxiety, I finally fell asleep when the sun came up. However, my sleep was light, and as soon as Jane walked in, I was up and awake.

She looked none the worst for wear and wore a smile as broad as a river and as lovely as a white dove.

"It is over," she said, just beaming with success. "We caught the assassin as he entered last night. He waited till the Lord looked like he went to bed and teleported in. Then to his surprise, he found the Lord armed and armored and me glowing in the room. I don't know what went through his mind right then but when his teleport scroll wouldn't work in my presence I thought he was going to faint. That is one young assassin who will thankfully never make Kings Choice."

Kings Choice was the fabled title of an assassin who had killed a King. None had reached it in over two hundred years, so it was a rare title.

"What about the man who hired him," I asked, 'we still know nothing about him?"

At that, she laughed, "by my Lord, I would have

thought you had figured that part out." I had not, and my blush must have given me away.

"I'm sorry Paden I didn't mean to put you down. I must admit that I left some information out that would have helped." I also had to admit the same thing, but my anger with her was way over. A full day and excitement had quelled it.

"That culprit was his brother." That statement was one of those moments you just wanted to slap yourself. Of course, there was only one person who could wish to see Lord Hampton murdered.

"That was why you wanted the Captain," I stated, understanding why he had rushed out after reading my letter. One Lord trying to kill another was a scandal that everyone would want to be kept as quiet as possible.

"Yes, I needed him arrested and figured the Guard Captain could persuade Lord Hampton easier than I. However it turned out to be unnecessary. Steven, the assassin, spilled his guts. Lord Hampton had his brother in irons before Joshua arrived."

"But why kill his brother if he would already give him anything he wanted," I asked though I actually knew the answer?

Jane answered, anyway. "Two reasons," she stated,

“he was broke again and his brother told him about the gold he found in the river. Lord Hampton is about to be a lot richer and was already cutting his brother off. Mathew Hampton, Lord Hampton’s brother, was about to be a lot poorer.”

Now the trips to the river made more sense, and the second to last issue was resolved. I only had one more question.

“What about Toby?”

She smiled even brighter if it was at all possible. “Lord Hampton only had one thing to say to him.”

“And what was that,” I asked?

“Get back to work.”

*Story 3*

# *The Stone Heart*

It is sort of funny how most people perceive the fighter's guild. They assume we spend every day fighting in life and death battles against impossible odds. The truth is far less glorious. Most days, we spend training, honing our skills till we are confident, physically fit, and ready.

Most missions involve little battle at all. Just take, for example, the quest at Lord Hamptons. The fighting was minimal. It is a model of most of the missions Fighter's Guild members face. Brains and planning often ended fights before they begin. Indeed that is the key to a long carrier as a fighter.

However, some Fighter's Guild missions do follow the perceived ideas. They take the mundane existence and turn it into something outsiders see as heroic. They are the eggs in which legends are born. And when we set off for our next quest, it was one of these that we faced.

It had been almost a month since we had stopped

the assassin at Lord Hampton's, and winter was more than halfway through. I had kept busy taking jobs with my new group. We had taken three missions so far and had done well.

First, we had killed a small band comprised of creatures we call a rous, also known as giant rats, down in the city sewers. Then we fought two enraged Ogres who had stolen a plow. Then lastly, we helped the guard catch one of their own.

It was the last one that caused us the most trouble. The guard had been blackmailing, stealing, and assassinating all over the city. He used his position to eliminate competition and gain wealth while he ran a reasonably successful crime ring. With the help of Captain Berkley, we rounded up most of his gang. Then with a long chase through the city, we captured the thieving guard.

Maria was the one who gets the credit for the actual act of capturing him. She jumped from a horse to drag the man from his. However, it was at the cost of her right ankle. She sprained it pretty badly, and the healers felt it best if it healed naturally.

Edward had also been injured. However, his was only a sizable cut that the healers had no problem closing. Still, I felt it best to give him a day to get over any possible lingering effects with one member down. In the meantime, I decided to take a small job for the night at a local Inn doing some guard work.

It was a cold, dreary night for southern Broma and freezing rain was possible. It would be miserable if it did, but at least I was heading for the warmth of the White Doe. I thought it funny that I was heading back to the place Jane and I had staked out not so long before. Twice now, I had visited Baker's district and ended up at the White Doe. It seemed connected to me somehow, and I felt they ought to give me a free room for the amount of time I spent there. Still, the owner remembered me from the Relics mission and had specifically asked for me for this night's event.

I was initially reluctant to accept. I hated the temptation of Alcohol. It was a sin I had given up, and the place would be practically flowing with it. Yet the money was good, and I didn't need a second person for the job. Therefore I went that night with just a sturdy wooden stick, my new mail shirt under a good woolen tunic, and over my poor thin gambison and my helm under my arm. I arrived on foot at the appointed time and entered the old beat-up inn.

It looked the same as the last time, with Blair standing there, washing out a glass, and grinning his ragged grin. He waved me over, and I walked to the bar to get my orders.

"I have a small concert tonight my friend and I could use a good pair of arms at the door," he said as he pointed to a chair that was already set up. "The singer also asked specifically for you. Wanted to give you a free concert," he continued.

"Thank you Mr. Cooper, and thank them also," I told him. I was surprised that I had been requested. I wasn't a well-known fighter yet, so it was a bit surprising to get a direct request.

I didn't want to waste time trying to figure it out though, I had work to do. I looked at the door and saw a place set up for me. The stool was situated so that I could see anybody coming in or out of the inn. It also kept me out of the line of sight for most of the observers so they wouldn't feel overly nervous at such an event. They would only see the two older barmaids that took the entrance fee at the door or the small stage that was already being set up with instruments. Mr. Cooper was obviously an old pro and, allowing for no rowdiness, this was going to be a comfortable 10 silver made.

"Just Blair to my friends Paden," Mr. Cooper replied back. "What would you like to drink and eat tonight? It's on the house."

"Tea and some of that stew you're maid just brought out, it smells good," I replied before asking, "Who's playing tonight?"

"The Angel," He said, baring his depleted teeth in a triumphant smile. I must have looked shocked as he continued. "Do you not think that one as well known as her would come to such a place to sing?"

I had honestly heard of The Angel several times

but had never seen her. Both trips I had made with Jane to the Grotto, which is the name of Normandia's amphitheater, had been to see Angel's contemporaries, but she was not playing. However, she was known to give charity concerts, and it was how she had acquired her name. It was also most likely why she had chosen this place to play and why she had invited me. It made sense that someone who liked to give charity events would reward the leader of a group who had just captured one of the city's most wanted with a free concert.

Still, I felt a bit guilty about being there without Jane. I had secretly acquired two tickets to the Bloom Festival. It was a concert Angel would perform at, and I had hoped to bring her with me. However, this was an excellent chance to see if the 15 silver a piece would be worth it.

"I am just excited to see her perform finally. I have heard a lot about her concerts and have wanted to see one for some time now."

The old man looked at me with a grin as if to say 'I know something you don't know' before telling me to get ready and getting back to work himself.

I took my seat and then started to work. The concert was an hour away, and for the most part, I didn't have to do much but watch the door. However, several band members came to the stage from the back rooms to look over the arraignments being made, and

I was surprised to see two of them that I knew.

One was Brother Thomas. An old abbot from a nearby village. The other was a 'disciple in training' Hoover Green. He was a small young lad who had taken to both faith and music. Jane had introduced me to both when she toured me around the chapel, and it seemed odd that The Angel knew them as well. I decided she must also be from the church and was a little hurt that Jane had not introduced me to her.

Then, once the crowd had gathered, the drummer came out. He proceeded to beat his drums for silence and announced that The Angel was ready. It was a massive crowd for such a small inn, and it took a few seconds to quiet down, but once it did, the band members started coming out.

The first person to come out to the stage were the musicians. Thomas was the lyre player and Hoover the flute. Both looked comfortable with the instruments in their hands. Then The Angel stepped out of the back room.

She was wearing a long white dress of flowing fabric embroidered on the sleeves with gold thread. On her waist was a golden belt of exquisite workmanship that matched the golden thread beautifully. The outfit was tasteful and yet set off her ample figure. Her long dark hair was braided down her back with gold thread. She also wore a hairpiece on the right side of her hair that offset the outfit perfectly.

Of course, I blushed at the sight of her. I never felt more foolish in my life. Here was the Angel on stage, and I knew now why Jane had never introduced her before.

At first, Jane didn't see me, but before she started her first number, she took a good look at the crowd. Her eyes spotted mine at the corner of the inn. I saw her smile heartily and witness Hoover say something to Thomas that brought a little red to Jane's cheeks. Then my food arrived, and the concert began.

"Prettiest singer in all of Broma," Blair said as he handed me the soup. It had been an hour since my order, but it was common to wait until the concert's start so that no one would see me eating. Like most good event planners, he felt it best that I ate when everyone would be looking elsewhere.

"You could have told me it was Jane," I said as I blushed slightly. "I feel foolish at being the only person in Normandia who didn't know."

"She is a very private woman and doesn't like to brag on herself," the innkeeper said as Jane's voice floated clear and robust to our location. She had a sweat high alto voice that would flow between smooth, clear vocals and a raspy, growly roughness at will. Her singing was not church music and held an excellent lively beat, but was clean and acceptable for even children to listen too. She also played the harpsichord with ease, and I sat there on my stool pierced once again to the heart by a woman I am not ashamed to admit I was falling for more and more each day.

The concert ended after two hours, and the crowd responded to her with waves of cheers. However, the night ended without incident, and I was glad to have earned my money the easy way.

After everyone had left, Jane came out and walked up to me at the bar where I sat talking to Blair.

“Hello Paden,” she said as giddy as a schoolgirl. “Did you like the concert?”

She had changed out of her white dress and was back in her more usual church robe, but I couldn’t help but feel how lovely she looked despite the plain new attire.

“Immensely,” I said in reply. Jane beamed at that. “Had I known you sang and danced so well I would have taken you to the New Year Festival.”

“I cannot,” she answered back as she sat down next to me. Blair had already poured her some whiskey. “Sally Beamer sings that every year and last year the crowd got me to play a few numbers. It was the talk of the town and upset Sally. She is too nice to tell me to back off so I avoid her concerts for the most part as to not overshadow her. She makes a living doing this; I just do it for fun.”

"Just for fun," I said, amazed. "How did you keep this from me this past month?" I asked, a little hurt. We had seen a lot of each other lately, and I knew we were becoming great friends.

"Easy," she replied as she downed her shot. I was a bit jealous to see her do so but fought down the urge. "You never asked."

I smiled. It was nice to know that Jane held secrets like this, and I felt the urge to pull each one out of her, but I fought it back. She was a friend, and I was scared to try to move any further along.

"So Joshua tells me you are leaving tomorrow for Ford Stanwald," Jane stated next. "They need a message sent north?"

I had been making it my business to spend time with all the people I might work with. I hung around Jane, of course, Old Man Gregory at the Fighter's Guild, the mage Trainer Quinaseria, an elf with incredible skill, and Joshua Berkley, captain of the guard. My time was starting to pay off, and I had just gotten my first mission referred to me by Joshua. Apparently, he had let the news travel to Jane.

"Yes, I am taking Eddy tomorrow and we should be gone for a little over a week."

"Maria's staying?" She asked next. The two lady's and

taken up a friendship and had seen each a lot during that time. If only Maria and Eddy could do the same.

"She needs to heal her foot," I replied.

"Then you will need to hire someone else," she stated boldly. "I have work north also so I will accept the commission."

Now I was stunned. "Hold on their Angel," I said, using her stage name. "You know I love your company and help but can the church and your fans live without you for a week."

"Of course," she said with a warm, playful smile she seldom used when in her Paladin persona. "I only do this for fun as I said. My real job will always be a Paladin and Soldier of God. If this interferes with that part of my life I would give this up easily enough. Besides, I have to go north with or without you."

"You are an amazing woman," I said before taking a sip of my tea. She blushed, but her face got serious, and she turned away. I had found when I talked to her in any way resembling flirting, she quickly shut down.

The silence lasted a few seconds before Hoover came out.

"Jane and Paden sitting in a tree," Both of us blushed

red as roses as Hoover passed by with his flute. Thomas was with him and tapped him on the shoulder with a disapproving look.

“Leave them alone boy, it’s rude to interfere with grownups.” He said sternly. “Tomorrow you have studies to get to and you need to be moving along.”

“Oh come on,” Hoover complained. “You’re the one who always said Jane is a fool with men and…”

Hoover never finished his statement. He was quickly grabbed by the ear by the old man. “That’s enough out of you young man.”

Thomas was red in the face. He quickly bowed to Jane and herded the young lad out of the building. Thomas was angry and mad, but he should have known better than to gossip around Hoover. Children never knew when to keep their mouth shut, and it was Jane that got hurt.

“That boy is a handful,” Jane said with a shake of the head. The giddy happy young lady she usually was when not working as a Paladin was gone. The fun-loving Angel was now replaced by the cold, calculating intelligence of Paladin Jane. “Gives poor Henry fits all the time.”

I couldn’t imagine anybody really giving the Grand Protector fits, but if anybody could do it, Hoover could.

"Well," I said after a few seconds deciding to get back to business and getting that miserable boy out of her mind. "The mission is just carrying a letter and the pay is minimal. Still, it is through Hunter's pass and I don't know if any goblins might get in the way. I will accept the help?"

"I will be at the guild first thing in the morning then," she said with a weak smile. It is evident that Toby's statement had hurt Jane deeply.

Jane was prompt, and if it wasn't for Eddy being a bit slow, we would have left before the sun had crested over the walls of the town. However, Eddy was lagging a bit that morning. Healing often drained the energy out of the person being healed, so he was a bit groggy. But we were not in a huge hurry, so we waited a few hours before we started off.

The nice part was that the sun was up and the traveling smooth despite the cold. No ice had formed the night before, after all, and the path was dry. The ride was brisk and quick, and in just five days, we made our way north to Stanwald.

The Fort was a small walled city that probably housed no more than two hundred people minus the merchants who wandered in from time to time. However, its walls were stone and tall and were garrisoned by some of the best archers in western

Broma. Plus, it was surrounded on the east by a large expanse of farming villages, and on the west were the mines that made it famous. The Baron was one of the richest in Broma, and he spared no expense when it came to protecting his people.

Our mission had been simple and successful. Take a letter to the garrison at Fort Stanwald was just an easy mission. As we rode up, it seemed as if this mission was nothing more than a pleasant ride north with two good friends.

I reached the garrison and handed off my letter to the guards. The guard thanked me and left. All I needed to do now was wait for my pay, and this mission would be over.

As we waited, Eddy, as usual, started talking. It was one of his most significant issues and his most annoying. Yet with nothing else to do, nobody complained. Neither Jane nor I said much back. It was hard to do once he got going, but the story was interesting. He talked about a duel he once was going to fight and how he waited six hours for the man to show only to chicken out at the last moment. It wasn't really that relevant. But Eddy seemed to feel silence was a sin.

I waited a few moments with the constant drone of Eddy in the background. I expecting the guard to come back with something to show we had completed the task. It was customary to get a receipt showing our work was completed so the guild could pay us. Instead, the guard came back with a Sergeant in tow. He looked grave and walked right up to me.

“I thank you for coming fighter,” He said as he put out his hand. He waited till we shook hands before he continued on. “We sent a letter to Normandia and Truinal asking for some reinforcements. It seems both Truinal and Normandia have declined.”

I couldn’t honestly know where he was going with this kind of speech, but something told me he would ask for my help right away.

“We have had a small bit of trouble and have lost one of our best cave units to a recent excursion,” he started. This interested me because Fort Stanwald was almost as known for its heavy spearmen as for their archers. They were specialists in clearing out goblins from caves, using the tight spaces and their phalanx to force the goblins into their spear points. “Five men went to clear an old mine that had seen some activity recently and before they even made the entrance they were attacked and badly routed. One came back and told most of his story, but his wounds were so bad that he has been out for days now and he seems to drift in and out of fever constantly.”

I was stunned. It must have been grievous wounds to cause a man to be out so long. I felt terrible for the warrior.

“It sounds like you need healers,” Jane said before I could speak. She had been a little more withdrawn on the trip, and anytime any conversation about relationships came up, she shut down into her Paladin serious persona. Once she went there, her emotions seemed distant, and she rarely added to the conversation. It was a new side of her and something I was learning to tread softly around.

“We have them,” The Sergeant said. “But the wounds were both poisoned and infected by the time we got him to the healers. It is beyond belief that he has lived so long but the healers feel he will pull through.”

“So now you are in charge of clearing out this cave and you don’t have other men who can help,” I stated, guessing where this was going.

“Truinal has had some minor riots in the last few months and most of our extra men are there.” The Sergeant said before spitting on the ground in disgust. “Stupid peasants think that the Truinal Witch has cursed the whole ducal family and that the new Duke is tainted. It is all just superstitious hogwash.”

“Peasants aren’t very bright,” Edward said in a low key. I shot him a glance, but the Sergeant took no offense. Obviously, he came from a noble family.

“Truer words were never said,” the Sergeant answered in reply. “But because of it I now have to attack a cave that has killed four and wounded one to his deathbed.

Yet all I have to accomplish this with are two other men. That is why I am telling you this story."

I didn't know if I should be excited or scared. I knew what was coming next. The Sergeant was going to ask for our help. Of course, I would give it, but I wasn't sure if this wasn't well above our capabilities. I almost wanted to laugh at the luck. The Truinal Witch may or may not have cursed the Truinal lords, but it seemed like a curse had been hurled at us.

"To think that Witch is dead and still doing harm," Jane said, still calm as day. The witch had been killed the summer before by two foreigners from Hammerfall. She had actually been the Duchess of Truinal, of all things, and had kept her evil well hidden. That was until a dwarf and gnome had exposed her. The story was still buzzing around the inns and taverns. It had become famous enough that bards had already made it into song. However, it seemed that her power had not entirely faded, even if it was nothing more than the power of fear.

"Yes it is, but that leads me to my question," The Sergeant said before asking the question we knew was coming. "Will you help us?"

"What is the pay?" I was surprised at the callousness of Eddy. It had never occurred to me to ask such a question, but Eddy had no such issues.

"What does it matter," both Jane and I blurted out

in response. However, the Sergeant answered Eddy's question without hesitation.

"200 silver per person and pillage rights."

I almost fell off my horse. 200 silver was good money, but pillage rights to any cave clearing could make some fighter's groups for life. These people really wanted help!

Still, this was very dangerous and a huge risk. The rewards could be substantial, but then again, it could amount to nothing. Worse could even happen as missions like this were as dangerous as they come. "We accept," I heard myself say before my mind had finished buzzing through the possibilities.

The Sergeant looked relieved. Obviously, he hadn't expected us to agree to this, and that would have meant going to the cave with just his men. Now he had doubled his ranks, and it was some relief to him.

"Good, I will have the private send word to the fighter's guild to let them know of your decision. Give me fifteen minutes to get myself and my men ready, and we can start for the cave. Leave your horses and unnecessary gear here. They won't be needed.

We agreed and busied ourselves with getting the horses unsaddled and put in the stables. By the time we had them comfortable, the Sergeant was back with his two men. It was a little nerve-racking to see such a small band, but it was all they had.

“I think in my haste, I haven’t given my name,” the Sergeant said as he came into the stables. He was dressed in a chain shirt with steel grieves and a steel helm. His shield was also metal-faced in the kite design, and his other weapons were a heavy six-foot spear and a war ax.

I looked at myself, and with the addition of my new chain shirt, I felt similarly armed to the three men who had entered the stables. It put a smile on my face for some odd reason.

“I’m Sergeant Blue,” he said. “The man to my left is Bruiser Bromberg and to my right is Bruiser Hooker.”

I shook the hands of the two newer guys before introducing myself, Eddy, and of course, Jane. With the formalities over, the Sergeant looked over our gear. Then once satisfied, we left for this old mine.

It turned out the biggest problem was finding this old mine. There were no maps to it anymore. It had been abandoned almost 150 years before and was only known to the locals by old papers in the Baron’s quarters. Had it not been for an escaped Kobbleman, a human who is a slave to goblins, the garrison at Fort Standwald would have never known goblins were near.

We hiked in the area for some time, looking for the entrance. It seemed like hours, and, as we had started late that day, the night was already beginning to creep in. All of us were getting nervous, as night always favored goblins, but the Sergeant had his orders, and he was prepared to search all night.

We had barely entered a small dip between two hills for probably the third time when an arrow shot out of the haze of sunset. I heard it hit metal and then heard a thud, but I didn't get to see who was hit. A small wave of goblins burst out of the woods to my left, and my attention was on them.

My focus first landed on the three hobgoblins in the background with bows cocked raining arrows down among us. All the goblins were on our shield side by the grace of God. Therefore I covered with my Targ and was lucky because I heard at least one arrow strike home.

I uncovered just long enough to see a Goblin warrior almost on top of me. He was only of Goblin rank, the second-lowest in their society. He was armed with a claw sword, a short sword that looked very much like a large cat claw, a rectangular shield, and leather armor.

He tried to grab my shield with his sword and move it out of the way, but his downward momentum carried him too fast, and he missed his swing. I had recovered from the shock of the ambush and bashed him hard with the boss of the shield. I heard him stagger while I raised my spear and stabbed forward. I hit him center mass, and he dropped like a stone.

I didn't get much time to recover, though. Two more were already on me, one from my right and then one from my left. I was furthest out in our group towards the enemy, and they were now focusing on me. The goblin on my spear side had closed the distance so fast that he was able to grab my spear and pull while the one on my left dropped kicked my shield. I stumbled right and went to one knee-knocking over the goblin that had a hold of my spear. However, he could still control his blade from his back and looked ready to slice my hamstring.

I didn't have time to react and knew I was about to be in serious trouble when an arrow struck that goblin straight in the chest. The goblin convulsed a few seconds and then died.

However, I had no time to watch as the goblin to my left was already on his feet. He was preparing to come down with his wicked sword on my head. He, too, was unlucky, however, as he was hit also. This time it was with a spear in the midsection. So intent was the goblin that he missed the Sergeant running forward and was impaled before he knew what hit him.

"Link up!" I heard Sergeant Blue yell. It was hardly needed. No sooner did he take my left flank than Bruiser Bromberg was on his shield side. We then formed a small shield wall and faced the remaining goblins. I didn't get a good count, but I heard the Hobgoblins still firing down on us and suspected around three of them. I also remember seeing at least as many goblins coming down the hill without bows as we had in our party. With three dead, that meant there were somewhere near 6 to 10 goblins still out there, so we were still at a disadvantage.

"I looked up to see two more goblins charge in. Both bravely tried to break through the wall, but with spears forward, it was suicide. I dropped one while the Sergeant did the same. Then I heard Eddie behind me firing a bow. The twang was music as it answered the bow fire from up the hill, and I knew it would at least make them take cover. Then a dart of fire shot over our heads, and I also knew that Jane was in the fight as well.

There was then a yell from up the hill, a gurgling kind of cry made when a shot hits its mark. Then another scream floated down more commanding, and the arrows stopped falling around and hitting my shield. I looked up the hill. Another goblin warrior was down with an arrow shaft through his gut, and up the hill, a hobgoblin was being dragged away, wounded by Jane's spell. Then they disappeared over the hill and were gone.

We stood in formation for a few more moments. The three spearmen, including myself, stood in front while Eddie and Jane stood in the back, ready to fire at any enemies that might want to try again. Then after a few seconds, we knew we could relax.

It took a second to remember that we should have had four spearmen, but Blue did not have any problems remembering. He was already heading back towards a figure lying on the ground behind us. I recognized him right away as Bruiser Hooker. He was hit in the chest and the bodkin arrow and punched through the chain like butter. Even though the fight was short, it was still too long for us to stop him from bleeding to death. He was dead where we found him.

“He was a good man,” Blue said as he looked down at him. He shook his head in disgust, but there was nothing to be done. Nobody said a word. We just helped Blue take him over to a nice area and lay him in a peaceful position, hoping we would be back to collect him in a few hours. Then we went up the hill and followed the goblins.

To our luck, one of the goblins was still moving. The last one Eddie had shot had been hit in the gut and had not yet died. We quickly got him well enough with magic to stand and then threatened him sufficient with death to get what we wanted out of him.

The frightened goblin quickly led us to the old mine, and soon we were standing in front of a large group of bushes. There was no cave-in sight, but the goblin swore it was there. We started to search around when I noticed Jane just standing looking lost. In fact, she had a faraway look like she couldn’t see anything around her, and I was actually worried that she had been hurt and didn't tell anybody. Then she suddenly started to glow. No sooner did the light touch the bushes than they shot up straight, and the cave was revealed.

"What the hell," Blue said as he looked at the cave!

"Exactly," Jane replied. It was then that I understood. Something evil was protecting the cave and had been trying to hide it. It was Jane's abilities that had saw through the rouse. Without her, we would have walked around for an eternity and never have found the cave. I was beyond glad I had accepted her help.

"You're a paladin," Bromberg asked, amazed?

Jane just shook her head yes as she started forward. Her mace was out, and the look on her face was all business. There was a knot in the pit of my stomach, though. Magic like hers came from God, and if it was needed to find this hole, only one thing could have tried to hide it. Demonic magic was at work here, and whatever we were about to face was possibly more than I bargained for. Still, what could I do? It was too late to turn back. I had made a commitment, and I couldn't back down. At this point, it was forward to glory or death.

"Wait up Jane," Blue said, catching her before she entered the cave. "We need a fighting order. You are too important, if this is a demonic cave, to be the lead fighter. Let the army take the point, with you and Paden second and Eddie reserve. “

She looked at him a second, still far away, and then came back to herself. “Yes, that may be best,” She said as she shook herself back to her surroundings. Her body language was cool and calm as always, but she seemed to be sensing powers we couldn’t see. “We do need to be careful though, my powers may be limited on unholy ground.”

“We have your normal magic I would figure, or was that fire dart something else,” he asked.

“Both Paden and I are mages,” she said with a matter of fact style. “But God’s powers have some advantages in caverns. I just hope I can concentrate hard enough to use them.”

“Anything is better than nothing. 4 goblins got away and there may be more in the cave. We may still be gravely outnumbered,” Blue stated back.

“The goblins are there but there is something else worse down there than goblins,” Jane said as if she was getting ready to take a stroll. How she could be so calm was beyond me. For me, the thought of worse made my hair stand on end, but Jane was immovable, as emotionless as stone.

“What about the prisoner,” Eddie asked as we started

to set up.

“Kill him, we don’t have time,” Blue answered back. Jane, however, had other plans.

“No,” Jane said quickly. “Tie him up. I may need him later.”

Blue didn’t argue. Paladins were a kind of priest, so who would kill something when a holy person told you not to. So the goblin was soon bound and gagged to a tree, and the group plunged into the mine.

The cave was obviously man made. It had no stalactites and stalagmites in it. Its chiseled walls and ceiling made walking easy, and we managed forward quickly through the first few rooms and hallways of the cave.

It was chilly and dark in the cave, and the air didn’t smell as I expected. I had figured rotting horrible smells would be pouring out, but the air seemed clean and clear as if we had been outside. I thought we would get lucky. There didn’t seem to be any signs of goblins. Then it was like the walls were alive.

Men, human men, seemed to blend out of the walls where their dark cloaks hid them. The ambush was quick and without warning. However, Jane, who was glowing minimally with the paladin light, sprang it out full force. I had seen her do this before, and it should have been brighter. However, it still did the trick. The enemy was blinded for a second, and it was enough time to get us ready for the onslaught.

Even so, the men were in amongst us quickly, and I found my spear being pulled from my hands before I could even bring it to use. Only my shield and knuckles kept them at bay as I tried to get my positioning with Blue. However, the men were only armed with daggers. We started having success, and several were down in just a few moments.

It was then that the goblins started pouring into the same hallway. We were squished and fighting on all sides. I finally got my ax out and dropped one of the men. Then I turned and was almost dragged down by another shabby looking Kobbleman.

He, too, dropped from the point on top of my ax. Yet the fight looked almost like a massive wrestling match more than a weapons fight. Jane was the only one who didn't have a goblin or man pulling at her. With shield and mace, she was bashing apart the lightly armored enemy and single-handedly forcing them back.

Still, it looked terrible for the rest of us until a wave of energy exploded from Jane and passed through the group. I didn't feel a thing, but the goblin standing near me looked like he had taken a kick in the stomach. It was all I needed, and I dropped him with a short chop to the neck.

The others also took the same opportunity, and the enemy started dropping like flies. The goblins soon found they were overmatched and started to try to retreat back down the hallway, but Jane had fought her way to Blue, and the two of them disappeared in a flash. Next thing I know, there is fighting up ahead of us as Jane and Blue were standing shield to shield, preventing their escape.

I knew Jane could teleport, so I wasn't overly surprised. However, the Goblins were. Several of the Koblemen and Goblins dropped their weapons, trying to flee as others fought on. Still, Eddie, Bromberg, and I came up behind them, closing off any escape.

The rest of the fight was brutal for the Goblins and their allies. Soon 10 men and 7 goblins were scattered throughout the hallway. All of us were cut and tired, but none of us mortally wounded. Only Blue had a severe injury as he had taken a shot to the muscle that connects the shoulder to the neck. This was on the shield arm, and he was having trouble raising it.

"We can heal that," I said as I started forward, but he waved me off.

"Save it," He said back though there was a grimace on his face. "We may need more of your magic in the near future and this won't kill me."

That was obvious, but we still took enough time for Jane to bandage it up. Then we put Blue in the back, and Bromberg and I took the point. We must have walked for hours, but time underground is impossible to keep track of.

“How big is this mine?” I asked after a long while.

“We left the mine about an hour ago,” Jane said calmly. “I assume they shut the mine down when they found the cave we have been walking around in. An old aquifer would be my guess.”

She was right. The ground was still smooth, probably from the water that had once been here, but now stalactites could be seen throughout the cave.

I was so focused on looking for goblins and traps that I had not taken the time to notice we had changed from man-made to natural surroundings. However, my few seconds of looking around almost cost me. I took a step back as I looked up above me at the higher ceiling. I stepped on a loose stone, and it slid away quickly. The next thing I know, there is a small pit with spikes opening up below me. Only Bromberg’s quick reaction kept me from a gut full of pointed sticks.

“That was dumb of me,” I said as Jane helped the Bruiser pull me back.

“We need to be careful,” The soldier said as I got my footing. I couldn’t have agreed more.

The rooms became much more significant as we delved into the earth, and soon we found ourselves in a cavern that had to be 30 yards in all directions. It was massive, and the floor was uneven. I didn't like it.

"We will have to be careful here," I said as I took the point. "This ground isn't good fighting ground and we could get hit by archers if they are hiding in here."

My voice carried a bit more than I liked, but we had not seen another goblin or Kobbleman since the fight near the entrance. Most of us thought we had gotten all of them. However, that would turn out to be a stupid assumption.

I hadn't crossed two-thirds of the room when I blundered into another trap. Two large rocks fell from the ceiling when I stepped on a pressure plate hidden on what looked like a step on the uneven floor. It had been made to match the rest of the floor, and I flat out missed it. However, I heard the clink as the metal wire let loose, and I rolled right to avoid whatever was going to happen. Bromberg did too, and we landed a few feet away from the rocks as they smashed hard onto the floor I had just been standing on.

I tried to pull myself up when my hand hit something different on the floor. I felt like a bone, and it was indeed. I was a bit surprised when the skull near it turned to look at me, and the eye sockets started glowing a wispy blue.

I felt the skeleton's hands come up and grab me as I peered into those eyes. I must have screamed the most blood-curdling scream I have ever produced. I had fought living men for many years, but I had never fought the dead up to that point. I feared them more than anything else, and at that moment, I saw my nightmare in person trying to make me his brother in death.

I tried pulling back, but it had me tight. Then the room started glowing as Jane once again let her light out. The skeleton obviously didn't like it and seemed to loosen just a bit of grip for a second. Terror had given me strength, and at that moment, it was enough. I pulled back and rained blows down with my shield. It busted the skull in several places, but each time it seemed to reform. I had no way of knowing how to kill it but didn't have time to figure it out. I noticed something charging at me from my left and had to split my attention.

At first, I thought it was Bromberg coming to my rescue, but to my horror, it was another dead goblin warrior. In fact, the room was full of them, and the whole group was once again fighting for their lives.

Instinct took over. I rolled to the only level ground nearby, which was to my right, and gained my feet. I managed to keep my shield in front, so I bashed hard at the new terror catching it flush. It had little weight having no flesh, and flew back from the blow, but the first one I had been smashing was already on its feet and had a nasty old sword in its hand. It was a sword, much like the goblin chopper, a falchion type sword, but much older in design.

It charged me, and I had just enough time to get my ax out before I was fighting it. I had little room to maneuver, but I was stronger than it and better armed. I managed to smash through its bones a few times, knocking it apart just in time. The other one was back up, swinging a similar sword at me.

This went on for a few moments. I would smash one apart just in time for the other to reform and attack again. Then I got lucky. One finally staid down, for what reason I didn't know, and I was down to one. However, this one changed tactics. It grabbed onto my shield so I couldn't smash it and just held on tight. When I tried to pull back, it sort of road my targ towards me and tried to stab me in the face. Luckily its sword was not designed to penetrate. It missed and glanced off my helm. Still, I couldn't shake it off.

I then stumbled while trying to back up, and I ended up with it over me. It rose up and was about to deliver a two-handed chop when a wave of indescribable force flew through us and shattered the skeleton to dust.

Again I didn't feel the blow that Jane had delivered. It didn't harm her friends, but I saw its effect. She was standing now on the highest ground shouting down at the skeletons, and each shout hit the undead like a sledgehammer. Some managed to stand through it, but most blew to dust. However, the two that survived her attacks were cut down quickly, and they didn't rise again.

I was still flustered when Jane came rushing up to me. Her usual calm demeanor was shot, and she looked distraught.

"Are you hurt?" She asked as she looked me up and down as if expecting to see blood gushing out of me.

"Only my pride," I said with a wary smile. "I scream like a little girl."

Jane hit me in the gut a little harder than she had meant to. "You scared the piss out of me and you're making jokes. Your pathetic Paden, you know that." The worried look had disappeared for a second as she allowed herself a relaxing smile. I had obviously worried her significantly, but a shout brought us a new set of worries, and in a flash, we were both back to business.

The shout had been from Bromberg but wasn't about more enemies. He was kneeling next to Blue, and there was no mistaking the anguish on his face. The Sergeant had actually taken the brunt of the fight. He had faced down four before Jane had blasted them apart. No one had seen him get hit in the throat, though. Yet the evidence was spilled all over the floor, and he was already stone dead.

Jane reached him before I did, but there was nothing we could do. We just stood there as Bromberg let his grief out. Two of our soldier brothers had already died, and I could tell Bromberg felt sort of alone being left with only us.

"He had two children and a wonderful wife," Bromberg said with tears flowing. "His littlest just turned two."

All of us felt the sadness, but Jane was crying right along with the soldier. She had been young when her father had died, and she, most of all, knew what this meant.

We were there for a very long time as we got his body to a less terrible place, and Jane made sure the evil of the site couldn't make him rise as well. Then we started off once again determined to end this evil.

We didn't have far to walk to find the end of it. At the end of the hall, we found another passage, and we could see a light. It was the only light we had seen, and we were convinced this was the end of the cave.

Bromberg had gone from sad to angry, and he was now the point man. I followed behind with Jane in the rear. Eddy would follow up from behind us all, but he had a large gash on the leg, and moving made it bleed badly. I wanted to heal it, but the evil of the cave wouldn't let me. We simply bandaged it the best he could, and the three of us were left to fight.

The end of the hallway led to another room smaller than the last. This one had sound footing and looked very much like a bedroom with multiple beds lining the walls. Standing in the middle stood three Goblins. One was the Hobgoblin that had burns from Jane's fireball from outside the cave; the other two were larger and had the gear common to slavers. We knew we had what we had come for, and there was no hesitation.

Bromberg and I both raised our spears to match the slaver forks the goblins carried. These were long two-pronged pitchforks used by slavers to help capture slaves. They also had a noose on the other end they could use to haul away their prisoners. They combined this with mooned shaped shields and linothorax armor. It made boogiemen dangerous and deadly opponents.

The four of us were soon fighting what amounted to a spear battle while Jane was fighting with the Hobgoblin she had already wounded. The match looked even and swayed back and forward for a little while.

My goblin was quick and was good with both his fork and shield. I had trouble reaching him, and he kept me at bay. Then we both started chanting spells, and are blows started sparking fire as both of us used our magic to try to get an edge.

Bromberg's goblin was doing the same, but Bromberg

couldn't respond with any magic of his own. It was a liability, and we had to count on Jane.

Her goblin was already injured, and I felt she should win that quickly enough. Once she did, we would have numbers. However, the goblins had other plans. All of a sudden, the lights went out. It was brief as Jane answered with her own light, but the room was still dim. Both good magic and evil magic were battling, and it looked like a stalemate.

This gave the goblin in front of me a few seconds. In my moment of confusion, he had left me and used the noose on the back end of his fork to grab Bromberg by the neck. Then the goblin held Bromberg for his friend, but luckily Bromberg was good. He used his greater strength to pull that goblin to him so that he could get enough play to dodge the other's attack. Then with the blunt edge of his shield, he swung wide.

The goblin trying to stab him missed, but Bromberg's shield didn't. It hit home on the other's helm and a sickening thud rung out. Then the room got a lot brighter, and the goblin with the noose flinched from the pain. This allowed Bromberg to pull the fork out of the goblin's hand and stab forward with it. The Slaver never saw his own spear pierce him. He was run through and just stared at the battle fork in his gut. It took a few seconds for the goblin to realize he was done, but the shock kept him from fighting back. He just collapsed to the floor and slowly started to die.

I turned to see Jane standing over the downed Hobgoblin, her mace having crushed in his skull. We had won! I couldn't believe it. We had been outnumbering three to one and with skeleton's to boot, but we had won. More impressively, Bromberg had killed both boogiemen without the use of magic. I started laughing as Jane shot me a smile. That faded as quickly as it came.

"Watch out!" She shouted.

I turned just in time to see what looked like a mountain of flesh running at me. My instincts saved me again as I rolled to my right. However, Bromberg was not as lucky. The Julton, a large kind of troll, rumbled past me and grabbed him with his hands. He then lifted the shocked man off the ground and pounded him on the ceiling a few times before winding up and throwing him hard against the wall.

Bromberg made a thud that sounded like half his bones broke as he crumbled to the floor. In the meantime, Jane had run at the troll from behind. She hit him as hard as she could with her mace. Yet the creature's fat and flesh held up, and it turned around backhanding her so hard she flew back five feet.

I got up and charged with my spear hitting it in the thigh as it tried to move. I noticed it had cuts and stabs all over it and had been injured at some past time. Yet the creature was so strong and angry that it was like fighting as if it was fresh. It grabbed my spear and pulled it out of itself before punching me in the shield. The force was like a sledgehammer, and I went stumbling back. Only the wall allowed me to keep my feet.

It then roared, and the foulest odor I had ever smelt flooded the room. Fear flooded me, and I noticed that Jane's light went out. This was what Jultons did. They used roars and stench to make opponents lose concentration. Jane had lost hers, and her light had gone out. However, the lights the goblins had put in the room still worked, and I could see the brute cocking my spear back as he swung it like a club. It hit me on the shield, but the shield buckled, and the spear slide into my gut. All the wind in my lungs was smacked out, and I am sure to this day that several ribs broke under the force.

Then the creature followed through with a powerful left-handed haymaker. That too hit home, and I don't remember the next few seconds. When I came to, the beast had Jane by the throat and roared at her while it lifted her up. Terror struck me, but I could barely move, then I heard the draw of a bow and the sweet twang of an arrow being released. Eddy had come!

The beast was hit in the back of the head. It was a great shot, but the thick skull kept it from being a killing shot. However, it was enough for it to drop Jane and stumble, confused as it looked for the new attacker.

The troll took a few seconds to orient itself, giving Eddy time to shoot again. He was so calm I could almost swear he was Jane's brother. The next shot hit the creature in the shoulder, and it didn't do much but piss it off more. It roared again, but with the blood loss it had from its old wounds and new ones, it didn't have the effect it had had the first time.

Eddy just drew his sword and stood his ground, waiting for it to charge into the hallway. It didn't get the chance. I managed to get to my feet and stumble forward. It saw me coming and turned to face me, fist, ready to fly.

To this day, I am not sure I would have managed to hit it if Jane hadn't also recovered, but she had and hit it from behind right in the back of the right knee. It buckled, and the creature fell heavy to its knees just as I struck for the heart with my spear I had just re-picked up. It was a direct hit, and the creature fell forward dead.

It was all I had, and I dropped to the ground hurting in the ribs. Jane was also injured as the creature had been strangling her moments before. It was Eddy who reached me first. His leg was still bleeding slightly, but he was the least damaged.

"Are you going to live?" Eddie asked, only half-joking.

"Thanks to you," I said weakly. Talking was pain, and I figured if it always hurt this much to speak, I would have no problem becoming mute.

Jane had regained her breath and was now on her feet. She looked at me, and I gave her thumbs up, then she walked over to Bromberg. I figured the man was dead, but when she reached him, I saw her say a few words into his ears. He moved slightly, but he was in no shape to do more. It was a fine group we made, and I was worried we wouldn't make it out of the cave.

"Can you heal him?" Eddie asked Jane as she walked by us again.

"Not with the evil in the cave." She replied as she headed to the back of the room. There was a nasty large bed in the back corner that had been the hospital bed for the Julton. Obviously, it had fought and destroyed the first group of soldiers and had received wounds for its effort. The goblins must have been trying to heal it for some odd reason. Those things ate humans and goblins. Still, they had not completed their task as they were obviously not adept at healing.

Next to the creature's bed was a stalagmite that had been carved into a round ball. It was smooth and creamy looking but was otherwise not impressive. However, Jane stared at it for a few seconds before coming over to me.

"Can I borrow your ax?" She asked.

"I shook my head yes," she took it from me, accidentally hitting my ribs. I grimaced in pain.

"I am so sorry," she said with a genuine look of concern. Jane could get serious when in a fight, but she was still a very caring person.

"What do you want it for?" Eddy asked as he re-tied his own bandage.

"That is the heart of the cave," she said as her smile faded, and a business-like attitude again resurfaced. "It is the reason we can't heal anybody."

"So you have to destroy it?" Eddy asked as she walked back towards the stone heart. "Why not use your mace," he asked before realizing her mace was in two pieces next to the Julton.

She didn't answer and didn't waste time. She walked with purpose right up to the stone and struck it hard. It took several shots but eventually, it cracked and fell apart. However, it did ruin my ax.

"I will buy you a new one," Jane said as she came back to me, throwing the ruined weapon on the ground. I would have told her she didn't have to, but it hurt to breathe.

She then bypassed me and went to Bromberg. She

proceeded to heal him enough for him to stand. He was still in bad shape, but he could walk. I was next, then Eddie. Soon we could all move, and we started our long walk back.

When we got to the Sergeant, we collected his body using sheets from the goblin's room and their battle forks to make a gurney. We also collected all the weapons and armor we could find on our way towards the entrance, putting them on a second gurney we had made using our own spears. It was hard for Bromberg and me to carry anything, so Eddy and Jane just dragged them to the entrance.

This was luckily not as far away as it seemed. The magic of the cave had actually been confusing us, making us unknowingly walk in circles. Once the heart was destroyed, we found our way without any difficulty. We got to the entrance with thanks and found our prisoner had escaped from his bonds and had fled. However, another surprise was there. Splash was standing there in his full saddle, waiting for Jane to come out.

"How in God's great name," I started to say when Jane shot me a look for using the Lord's name in vain.

"He is a Paladin's horse Paden. He knows when he is needed." She answered back before we loaded him up with the weapons and the Sergeant's body. Then we collected Hooker's body and walked the miserable miles back to Standwald. Luckily the sun was already up, and we had no trouble finding the trail.

When we got their all four of us collapsed into cots and spent the next two weeks in the care of the Baron's healers, free of charge.

As I said in the beginning, most fighter's guild missions didn't have a lot of fighting but those that did make the fighter's who lived through them Heroes. From that day on, Jane and the Fighting Quoins carried that title, for better or worse.

*Story 4*

# *The Bloom*

Nitesco is the first month of the year, and the 1st of Nitesco is also the first day of spring. For southern Broma, this means rain, rain, and more rain. The weather is chilly, and the sky is usually cloudy. The rain comes down in heavy torrential downpours and drenches everything for at least half the month. However, the rain never seems to start before noon. Then the sun does its best in the morning to evaporate all the rain from the day before. This kind of weather was typical for Broma and exactly how Nitesco 1st was my first year with Jane.

The 1st is also the start of the Bloom Festival, the Broman New Year, so it is no surprise that everyone was up early to beat the monsoon and get some celebrating in before the rains could start. Parties spread around the country like wildfire, and everyone came out to gather and socialize after the cold and dull winter months. It was many people's favorite holiday, and it was easy to understand why.

In southern Broma, the weather was usually brisk

but not freezing. Cool enough to frost our breath but not cool enough to frost the ground. That was chilly enough to warrant gigantic bonfires to keep areas warm and allow colder participants to warm up. There were also street bands on every street corner and the porches of every café. They were singing and dancing in happiness that spring had arrived. This year was warmer than average in temperature, so it was worth getting up and out.

The amphitheater also held music and plays for as long as the weather stayed nice. It was one of the rare times they lowered their prices so that most of the public could afford to come. Everyone from the city would flock there. It was when the big names came up to sing or perform that the place would get crowded. It was one of my favorite parts about The Bloom Festival, and I loved to go out and see the shows. However, this year was even more special. I was in Normandia for the first time during the party and was excited to see how the Capital celebrated the holiday.

The King of Broma and his family always started the show in Normandia ever since his kids had come of age and learned to play instruments. That year was no different. He played a horn very well while his son played several woodwind instruments, his daughter played strings, and his son in law played drums. It was the only time they played together in public and was worth the price just to get a glimpse of the royal family.

Of course, with all this going on, I was up and out early. I had two tickets to burn and wanted to get a good seat. Besides, Jane was part of the entertainment, and I wouldn't have missed her perform for all the gold in the world.

Maria was a lot better and was able to come along as well, so I didn't have to waste my second ticket. It was nice she had healed so quickly, and I was anxious to get her back into the field. It had been some time since any of us had worked, and I couldn't wait to get The Quoins up and fighting again.

I had asked Eddie and Jonny Bromberg if they had wanted to tag along, but the boys didn't want to come. They had decided to buy equipment that morning and would be busy all day spending my money.

I didn't mind. Jonny had joined me after getting an honorable release from the army. He needed equipment, and I didn't have extra's to give him after selling all the goblin gear from the last mission save one slaver fork and moon shield. With this problem in mind, they had set out with most of what was left, around 2000 silver, and were determined to get him ready.

Luckily the 1st was always a good time to buy gear. The reason was that The Bloom Festival had one other attractive little benefit to it. It was the eve before Broma's second festival of the year called The Cull.

The Cull was when Broma's lords would raise the bounty on all the dangerous animals that lived in the area for one day. Because of this, the shops that sold weapons had taken to giving huge discounts during the Bloom festival, and Jonny and Eddie had gone to take advantage.

Of course, none of this was on my mind when Maria and I made it to our seats early enough to see the King start the show. I was just ready to relax for one day and enjoy the warming of the weather.

Many nobles didn't like the royal family participating in the festivals. It seemed frivolous to many of them and made the festival harder to guard. Still, the royal family endeared themselves to the peasantry with their yearly performance, so they ignored the Lord's advice and did the show anyway. I, for one, was happy they did.

The royal family didn't disappoint. They played very well and kept the crowd entertained. The princess was incredibly skilled at music, and it was her solos that received the ovations from those watching.

Next up was a small group of acrobats. They were great rolling and jumping and doing all kinds of physical feats. They were so good that we got tired of cheering before they got tired, jumping around and making everybody's' jaws drop.

Then there was a magician. He did fire spells and light

spells and even some sleight-of-hand. His act was even better than the acrobats, and many of his tricks and spells got standing ovations greater than either of the other two actions.

Then it was Jane's turn. I would have easily put it as the best of the day, but Maria said I was biased. Either way, Angel did get a standing ovation. However, it didn't last long. No sooner did the clapping start than it started to sprinkle. Soon that sprinkle turned into a downpour, and everyone ran for shelter, thus ending the shows for that Bloom Festival.

I was one of the last ones undercover as Maria was still using a cane and was babying her ankle a little bit. I helped her to one of the nearby cafes' pavilions that were prevalent around the amphitheater. The current family of Kings had brought the concept of diners from the country of Amor, and they were trendy in Normandia. With the rain coming down as it was, it was even more popular than The Bloom Festival.

I hadn't reached the pavilion for more than a few seconds before I realized that familiar faces were also taking shelter there. Captain of the Guard Joshua Berkley was standing shoulder to shoulder with Quinny, my magic instructor. His real name was long and hard to say because he was Elvin, so everybody called him Quinny.

"Another perfect Bloom festival," Quinny said to Joshua with what I took to be just a hint of disgust.

“I prefer the night of lights we Elves celebrate at the start of spring. At least it usually doesn’t rain at night in the heart of Sari.”

“The rain is part of the attraction,” Joshua said with a smile as two teenagers went running through the streets behind us, laughing and screaming pleasantly through the rain. “It’s a time for the earth to renew and for crops to start growing.”

“And for kids to do naughty things they shouldn’t,” Quinny said, still giving the sky an evil look. “And soak unfortunate wizards.”

“I forgot that you melt in the rain,” Josh jested at Quinny with a mischievous grin. Quinny looked at him with an evil look, but the threat was a hollow one. His face soon broke into a grin, and both of them starting to laugh.

“You are as big a pain as the rain,” Quinny accused Josh. “I’ve never a more troublesome student in all my years.”

“Worse than Paden,” Maria chimed in, taking the opportunity to tease me? Quinny was the headmaster of destruction magic and magic battle theory at the local Mages’ guild and had taught both myself and Joshua.

“Of course,” Quinny answered back. His face wasn’t

all that serious looking. Quinny often acted seriously, but he was pretty fun-loving once you got to know him. "They both are hopeless with magic, but at least Paden respects his teachers."

Being called hopeless was a good thing with Quinny. It meant he liked you. It was when he gave you the 'very good start over' line he was famous for that you had to watch out.

"Who knows what tomorrow will bring," I replied also. "Maybe I will surprise you."

Joshua seemed to misinterpret that line. "So you are heading out to the Cull?"

"No, I plan to..." I would say stick around a little while longer and wait for Maria's ankle to heal fully, but it never came out. Instead, I was interrupted by a plea.

"Paden, I need your help," another voice said, sounding distressed. Jane came running in followed closely by Hoover' a priest in training and one of Jane's band members'.

Her hair was dripping wet as water flowed down her braid. Yet it was her traditional singing dress that was gathering attention. It was soaked through and hung to her curves like a second skin. More importantly, it was white, and most of it was easily see-through. Only her girdle kept imagination alive.

“Jane,” I said, my face as red as a rose. “You’re practically naked!” Luckily I was carrying my rain cloak, which I took off quickly and put on her shoulders.

“Yes,” She said, blushing intensely and sounding completely flustered. “But my cloak is missing and since the rain is so heavy I was getting wet under the pavilion. When I saw you I thought you might loan me yours.”

“So he has,” Josh said, as Jane put my cloak around her tight. “Why don’t we walk you over to the church and get you into something a bit more modest. And Hoover, I am disappointed in you. You should have offered her your cloak like Paden did.”

“Then I would have gotten wet,” Hoover said with a sly smile as he walked to the edge of our shelter, getting ready to brave the rain again. “And also missed the view.” With that, he darted past all of us laughing and ran into the shower to find his friends.

I looked at Jane, and she glared at him. She wasn’t so modest that she would pass out of embarrassment, but she did like to keep her wholesome reputation. I pitied Hoover when she got a hold of him next.

“I am going to tan that boys hide,” she said as he ran out of sight. “I thought we had taught him better.”

“At least one man still knows manners,” Maria said as she too watched the boy run out of sight. “Paden at least knows better than to gawk at women.” I didn’t want to tell Maria that I would have loved to keep Jane standing there in that soaked through dress, but even a mage like Quinny would have been hard-pressed to make me say that out loud.

“Quite so, but it is over now and I do feel that Josh is right,” Quinny said. “We should get her out of the rain and to a location where she can change.”

“Thank you, gentlemen, really, but I feel Maria can get me there just fine,” Jane said. She looked flustered, which was a side of her hard to produce. “Besides, right now I have a sudden urge to hide in my room and never come out again.” She was on the verge of tears, and I instinctively put my arms around her. She put her head on my chest, and for a few seconds, we stood there, her shivering in my arms while I held her. Then she caught herself and pulled away.

“Will you be kind enough to take me back Maria?” She asked. Maria shook her head, yes, and the two of them walked off towards the church moving as quickly as Maria’s bum ankle would allow.

“Well that was interesting,” Quinny said as he looked back at us. He was Elvin, and a human woman was frankly beneath him. Even Jane could barely turn his head.

“Yes, she should have known not to forget her cloak,” Joshua said with a grin. “She has started to get distracted lately.”

“Women do that when they get involved,” Quinny said as he shot me a glance. I wasn’t sure what they were talking about, but Joshua continued.

“Very likely,” Joshua said. Then he saw my expression and changed subjects. “Hear about Tyson’s farm.”

“Yeah, Lord Franklin is offering 50 silver a pop for spinney funguses. Seems the farmer has gotten an infestation of them and there aren’t enough blue hornets this year to cull them,” Quinny replied. He had to throw in the blue hornet statement. He loved to show everybody just how much he knew.

“They should have gotten the fighter’s guild involved earlier but I guess it is better late than never.” Joshua continued. “However it will make the Cull interesting. There will be a lot of new fighters heading out trying to bag one. I feel a little apprehensive as it will mean that my guards and healers will be out in force dealing with injured men.”

“Spiny funguses aren’t really that big a deal.” I chimed in. “If you have a pavis shield and a crossbow you can kill them easily enough.”

“Yes Paden, but you’re experienced and most of those

out during the cull are first-timers," Josh said back. "Are you even planning to go out yourself? It is 50 silver a fungus."

"He said no earlier," Quinny started, but then he looked at my face and saw my thoughtful expression. It was obvious what I was thinking. Fifty silver Bromans was a lot for such an easy target. I, of course, then hesitated on my reply.

"I stand corrected. He wasn't originally planning on it Josh, but it looks like he might now," Quinny laughed. "It is good money if there are as many of them as the Tysons say?"

This statement also piqued my interest. If there were just ten funguses, then we were already looking at excellent money. However, if there were 20, which did happen from time to time, that could be worth my time.

"Unsure how many of them, but they did say it could be a mob," Joshua said, shaking his head. A Mob was somewhere near 50, so it sounded like a great chance for good silver, but that scenario was rare as a farmer would have to be incredibly careless to allow so many without calling in the fighters to end the issue. I wouldn't take stock in a Mob. I could believe a herd of 10 or more, but a Mob no way.

"Maybe I will look into it," I said as I thought about the idea. I was doing well for my first year as the money had been coming inconsistently. I had already paid all my fighters a year's room and board, except Jonny, who was new. So at this point, everything else I made was a profit for my group. A few more silver Bromans would be lovely, and I was getting excited at the possibility. If there were as many as they claimed, I could make some real money and finally get myself a good horse.

I was standing inside the church only a little while later when Hoover came down from the upstairs walkway. His face let me know somebody applied punishment for letting Jane run around in a white dress and pouring rain. It looked like whatever the sentence was, it was likely to work.

I waited a few more seconds when Maria came downstairs. I waved at her, and she came over.

"Here's your cloak," she said as she came up to me. I thanked her as I took it. Then looked at her with her hair all stuck to her head from the rain. Lucky for her, she had been wearing brown linen and wool and hadn't had to worry about showing off.

"How is she," I asked?

"Fine, now that she is dry," Maria said. She had a grin on her face that was sort of weird but then clarified the expression. “Since we met her I was starting to think she wasn’t human. But it seems even she can get flustered.”

“How did she forget her cloak,” I asked as shook my head? “She is usually very organized.”

“A conspiracy from the disciples in training,” Maria said, still with a grin on her face. “It’s a ritual. They convince one of the newer members to take something of their elders as an initiation. They convinced Hoover to pack her cloak and then hide it.”

“And they got in trouble also I take it,” I said, shaking my head.

“Not at all,” Maria said with a small laugh. “Its tradition in the church to do this. The secret is that they are supposed to suppress the urge to follow through. It’s a test, and Hoover failed.”

“Not a great secret initiation if they just tell anybody,” I said back.

“They don’t. As we are adults we wouldn’t get such a test if we joined. Therefore they don’t care if we know,” Maria finished off. “You know she is going to prayer so if you are going to talk to her you will need to do so now.”

"Ok," I said with a smile. "Just do me a favor and as soon as you see Eddie and Jonny let them know I need two pavis shields and crossbows. They can rent them from Ozzie, he has some."

"Why," she asked, confused.

"We are going out tomorrow," I answered back before leaving her and heading up the stairs towards Jane's quarters.

It was early enough that men were allowed into the Maidens' wing, but I always felt odd going down their hallway.

Jane's room was midway down the hall, and I reach it right as she was coming out. She was now in her typical church robes and had dried off pretty well. It was odd just how lovely someone could be even in loose, shapeless robes and damp hair.

"Hey Angel," I said with a smile. Her back was to me, and she almost started when she heard me. She was still flustered.

"Hello Paden," She said back with a small smile as her hand instinctively brushed her hair back from her face. It was funny how she seemed to do that a lot when I was around. "I didn't thank you for loaning me your cloak. It would have been extremely unpleasant to walk back here without it."

“It was hard to give it up and miss the view,” I said with a wink and a smile. I was trying to be playful. What was the harm with nobody around but as usual, I should have kept my mouth shut?

Her body language instantly changed. “It’s not funny Paden,” she said on the verge of screaming at me. “I was half naked in front of the entire town. My reputation and honor were at stake and you have to act like a pig when I was trying to compliment you.” She emphasized pig to let me know just how she felt right now. “I frankly expect better from you,” she said as she was on the verge of tears again. “Why do you men all have to be such dogs!” She slammed her bedroom door close and started to walk off.

“I’m sorry,” I said as I started to chase her down the hall. “I shouldn’t have said that. I apologize. I was just trying to be funny.” I knew that was the wrong thing as soon as I said it.

“Paden,” she started in frustration. I had never seen her this way and didn’t know how to react. She was both upset and angry and was so flustered she couldn’t finish her statement. My instinct was to reach out and hold her again, but she pushed me away. “Just go Paden.”

“Sorry Jane,” I said again. “I really came up to let you know I am going out tomorrow for the cull and wanted to know if you would come.”

"Not this time," she said, still angry. "You have Maria to stand there and look pretty for you since that seems to be all you men care about." Then she stormed off down the stairs and to the main chapel with me standing there like an idiot.

Now, as you already know, all the stories I am telling here include Jane, but when my group and I were walking down the road towards Tyson's farm, all I could think about was how I had blown it with her. Childish, I know. Jane was never so petty as to throw away a friend over one stupid comment. But I was frankly still a child then, and my fear had the best of me.

To make matters worse, Maria and Eddie were at each other's throats all morning. The argument had started innocently enough. Maria had commented about Eddy being hard to wake up in the mornings. She didn't mean anything by it, but Eddie had taken it as a comment about his character. Then the harassment about being a peasant had started.

I had tried twice to shut them both up, but that was like trying to dam a river. Both hated silence and neither ever backed down. Maria could be shy when she first met a person, but her more aggressive side would come out after that. That was a bad combination with Edward's self-perceived status and stubbornness.

We had been trying to decide how to approach Tyson's farm. Most knew that funguses could see people coming from any direction and shot their spines without much provocation when in large groups. We had been trying to determine if it was best to go by road or field. The road was nearer to the houses and might mean we get too close. However, the crop field would mean we would have to walk a lot farther to get there. Maria had just given her opinion. She favored the field when Edward, who disagreed, started in on her once again.

"I don't care what a peasant thinks," Eddy said as we passed Johnson's Farm. It was a typical Broman Farm. One large manor house surrounded by dozens of small two-room shacks. These were lodging for the workers while a large barn housed the animals. There were also two-grain towers. But I saw none of it as my temper had pretty much reached its max.

"That's because you're too pompous to know good advice when you hear it," she bit back.

"Stick to sowing and cooking woman," Eddie retaliated, taking it way, way too far. "Leave the fighting to the..."

He was going to say to the fighters, I was sure, but my anger had exploded. "Eddy, one more word out of you and you are fired," I practically screamed! A good leader stays composed, but I had lost any sense of calm the day before. I convinced myself Jane would hate me forever, and I took it out on Eddy and Maria. "And that goes to you as well Maria. I have had enough of the two of you fighting like cats and dogs."

Both glared at each other. It was a situation I knew would only get worse unless I could teach Eddie to respect her. If not, someone would have to get fired indeed, and I didn't have the workforce to do that just yet. The problem was Eddie knew it.

"Whatever boss," Eddie said back to me as he quickly passed in front of us and put enough distance between himself and us to end the fighting. I should have fired him for that. After all, I did say 'not one more word.' However, I just glared at him as he walked ahead like a lord in front of his servants.

Maria, on the other hand, slowed down and got behind Jonny. He, too, was a bit prejudice against peasants, but he had enough class to give anybody a chance.

"So what should we do," Jonny asked?

I shot him a glare too. My mood was very foul, and I was not myself. Then I caught the look he gave me as if I had wounded him, and I took a deep breath.

"We are almost there already so I figure we should just stick to the road," I said with too much bite. Jonny didn't say anything. He was a soldier and would follow orders. Maria, on the other hand, seemed to take the news as an insult. In hindsight, she was right, but I was too angry to think. Luckily she kept her mouth shut.

The rest of the walk was pretty quiet. Nobody talked as I brooded over Jane, and Eddie and Maria brooded over each other. It must have been an excellent example for Jonny coming on his first official trip with us. I still feel to this day he would have quit had it not been for our previous adventure back at the Stone Heart Cave.

Still, work soon was able to take our minds off our troubles. We found our first fungus about two miles out from the farm and killed it. It was easy as spiny funguses are vulnerable if they can't shoot you. An easy kill was precisely the case for this fungus due to the pavis shields. In seconds Maria and Eddie had shot the beast to death. We had the first proboscis to take back as proof.

It didn't take long to kill three more, and I started to feel good about the day when we finally made it to Tyson's farm.

"By the Angels in heaven," Eddie said first! I had to agree. There in front of us was the farm, just like a typical farm in Broma. There was the farmhouse, barn, small huts, and a grain silo. Yet even from several hundred yards, it is evident that there was fungus everywhere on the grounds.

"There must be at least a hundred plus fungi," Maria said in response to what we were seeing. She had just started to limp badly again and was using my spear as a crutch. However, as the best shot we had, I had still taken her with us.

"We don't have enough bolts," Jonny chimed in as we stared at the manor house. The worker huts were far out near the fields and didn't seem to have an issue. But the barn and manor house seemed to have small herds of the creatures everywhere.

One hundred creatures were a small estimate. I could easily see 150, and the manor house was blocking most of our view. Who knew what the silo held on the other side of the house.

"I have heard of Mobs but never thought I would see one," Eddy said. I again had to agree. Fifty beasts were considered a mob, but 150 would be a super mob. Hell, I had never even heard of that many in one place in any story I had ever heard. It dumbfounded me that nobody had come out here sooner to solve this problem.

"We can't go near that place," I said as I looked at it. We were all armed and armored, but with gambison on Jonny and Eddy and Linothorax on Maria, there was no way they could risk going in. We only had two pavis shields. If a shot came from something other than head-on, it would get through. With poisoned spines, this was just too risky.

“Agreed,” Eddy and Maria said in unison. Both looked at each other like it was rude for the other to have the same thought, but they let it drop.

“Then we will need to back up and pick some off as they come out. Later we will need to report this to the town guard and see if there is anything we can do from there,” I stated as I turned around to find a better place to set up and ambush a few more fungi. That was when another shock appeared.

Jane was riding up the road on Splash and heading straight for us. I didn’t expect to see her and the shocked look on my face made everyone else turn around.

“Jane,” Maria said, a bit surprised as well. We all waved, and soon Jane was riding up to us.

“Didn’t think you wanted to come,” I said when she got into hearing range.

“I was asked to come out in search of a few missing boys,” she replied in her normally calm persona. It was the Jane I knew best as she was all business when there was business.

“What do they look like,” Jonny said before anybody else could ask the obvious question?

"Bobby Monday is their leader and he is Maria's age. He stands about a quarterstaff tall," she said as she looked at the manor house. Even her familiar cool composer looked shocked at the sight, but her voice didn't reflect it. "He has dirty blond hair with light blue eyes and medium build. You would recognize him best as one of the horse trainers out at Monday's ranch."

I had been going out the Monday ranch for a few weeks already and had been trying to find out what a good horse would cost. I had seen Bobby there and knew his looks.

"He is also with Greg Little and George Holler," She continued. "Greg is a blacksmith apprentice and a large lad in girth and height. George is a peasant from a nearby farm and is shorter than the other two with dark hair and eyes. Their girlfriends all say they came out here with nothing more than short swords and daggers."

"Were they coming to this farm," I asked? If they were, we might be doing a body rescue.

"Yes," she replied to my horror. She looked me in the eye, and I could see the concern there. She knew just how bad it might be when she saw the manor.

"I guess we are going in after all," Edward said as he too looked back on the house. It was apparent he also was scared, but you could never have called Eddy a coward.

“No,” I replied as I took the crossbow from him. He looked at me like I had gone mad. So did Jane. I guess they figured I was going to abandon the boys, but that was not my character. “But we only have two pavis shields. Jane and I will risk it alone.”

Jane let break a smile, but the news didn’t sit well with my group.

“You have got to be kidding,” Jonny said! “You will get killed trying to take on that many.”

“I don’t intend to take on any if I can help it,” I replied as Jane got off the horse, and I took the pavis shield that Jonny carried. “I intend to get to the house and use it to cover our backs. Then Jane and I will get to the front of the house and see if there are any bodies. If we are lucky the boys thought better than to try to kill one of these creatures and have just left.”

“I don’t like this boss,” Eddie said as Maria handed Jane her crossbow and limped away, still holding my spear. “It is just like a bunch of peasants to put themselves in this much danger.”

“How many times do I have to tell you, Eddie, not to talk like that,” I scolded. It was a weak comeback as my mind agreed with him. Peasants were always getting us into danger, but that was why we had a job to assist Broman citizens.

“Sorry boss but it is the truth,” Eddie said as he walked up to me and put his hand on my shoulder. “I take it you will want us to tell the guards what is going on here.”

I shook my head, yes. He was a pain in the ass, but Eddie was not stupid.

“Take Splash back too,” Jane said as she came to stand next to me. “He would surely get killed trying to go where we are about to.”

Maria had no problem with that. Her ankle was throbbing, and she wanted off it. Jane handed her the reigns, said a few nice words to the horse, patted him on the nose, and watched as the rest of the Quoins left.

“Can you sense anything,” I asked her as we started towards the house. Our shields were in front of us, and we were moving slowly, trying not to startle anything.

“These are creatures Paden, not evil creatures,” she replied. “Your sensing spell would be better suited than my evil sense.”

I still didn’t understand all her powers, but I

understood her sensing would not help us here. As far as my sensing went, I could use it to try to find the boys, but I wanted to be closer to the house before I tried.

The walk to the house was nerve-racking. I had never seen anything like it before, and I didn't honestly know if this idea was good. Anything coming up to the house that wasn't in full plate armor was like to be killed by the spiny monsters. Yet there I was attempting to approach without anything other than a pavis shield and mail armor. It was stupid, and I was frustrated I had found myself in yet another ridiculously dangerous situation.

We reached the back part of the house without a hitch. As I look around, I got a good look at several of the creatures. It seems like a mix between a brain coral sponge and deer moss for those who have never seen a spiny fungus. This fifty-pound ball like mushroom also carries around 100 eight-inch spines sticking out in almost every direction. They have spindly legs that look like sticks and a hollow proboscis to suck the juices out of plants and animals. They can even distort their bulbous bodies to aim their spines with eerie accuracy. They do all this without having any eyes at all.

The ones at Tyson farms were hard at work, eating everything. They were sucking trees dry. Several animals and birds had shared that fate. The creatures were so numerous that they stuck to the outside of the house. They were draining the barn wood walls to the point they already started to look dried out. It was the most unique and terrifying thing I had yet seen.

Yet it was only about to get worse. Soon we were on the side of the building heading for the hidden front when Jane put her hand on my shoulder.

"What is it," I asked as we stopped. Her face looked far off as if she was sensing something I could not.

"Remember when I said my powers would not be useful in sensing," she said as she turned to look at me. Her face wore a hint of surprise.

"This can't be good," I replied, knowing what she meant.

"Something evil is nearby within 100 yards or so."

It was news I didn't want to hear. "Great, not just a mob of fungus but possibly undead fungus as well," I said, as I looked over at Jane and smiled. She laughed back.

"Only you could joke during this," she replied.

The creatures seemed to be still ignoring us, so we decided to go around the corner and take a good look at what we were facing. In all the years I may live, I will never forget the sight.

As I said earlier, ten or more funguses are a herd, fifty, or more, a mob. However, what we saw when we turned the corner had no name till that date. Pouring out of the silo and filing the area between the barn, house, and silo had to be over 1000 funguses!

To put that in perspective, Jane and I each carried 24 bolts for our crossbows and could shoot maybe four magical spells that could kill a beast. All said, that may mean we could take out 56 creatures before we had to go to ax and mace. That would leave over 944 funguses to deal with, assuming we didn't miss a shot. There was no way we could end this mess.

"Oh, shit," was all I said as I scanned the place. Even Jane, who typically wore a mask of calm, looked surprised enough to go speechless. Then the creatures who had let us get that far decided they wanted something else to eat.

The first shots came from the creatures on the walls. It was a good thing they started the show as our shields faced them. They held up well against the first bolts and gave us time to act. We quickly realized we were in trouble and went right back around the side of the building as an unbelievable barrage of spines flew by.

"Oh shit," I said again as we crouched against the wall behind our shields. It was a good thing pavis shields are the size of a half door. The creatures that had let us pass were now interested, and the twenty or so on that side of the building started heading in or direction, shooting as they came.

Both Jane and I started firing back. Jane unleashed fire as I unleashed electricity. However, after I hit the first one with a bolt of electricity, I thought the fire was a better choice. It hit the creature and killed it, but the bolt caused its spines to release and the air quickly filled with spines.

"Do that again," Jane said as she switched from the fire. I was confused at first, but I saw many creatures stuck with the spines from the one I killed when I looked out onto the field. It was like setting off a Dwarven landmine.

We quickly exhausted or electric spells, even getting lucky enough to have one of the spells branch off and hit three for the price of one. However, it was like trying to empty the ocean with a bucket. The creatures were crawling over each other to get to where we were. I was just about to sound the retreat when I heard voices screaming at us.

From out of the manor house came the sound of two of the boys trying to get our attention.

"We can let you in if you hurry," one said. I recognized the voice as Bobby's.

I couldn't believe they were still alive, but they

wouldn't live long if we didn't get to them soon. The creatures were devouring the house itself, and at some point, the walls wouldn't hold.

"We have got to get to them," I said to Jane, who just shook her head in agreement.

We both then got behind our shields and started back around the corner. Jane had her shield in front as she was in the lead. Mine covered our side. I was hoping we had killed enough of them behind us to keep us from getting hit, but as we pushed our way into the house, I felt a sharp pain in my left leg.

The poison burned as I started to fall, but Bobby pulled me in as his friend slammed the door shut behind me. I grabbed my leg and felt that the barb went all the way to the bone.

"Your hit," Jane asked with real concern. It matched the time skeletons had attacked us during the stone heart. Yet this time, she had reason to fear.

"Yes," I said as I dragged myself away from the door. At the same time, the man I figured was Greg pulled a table back in front of the door. He looked injured on his right shoulder, and I could see he had lost some of his strength in it. Then I looked to my right and saw Bobby favoring a leg and George lying on another table covered in blood and barely breathing.

"I can heal you," she said as she calmed down quickly and started to examine the spine.

"George first," I answered as I pointed to the table. She missed George's condition in her concern for me, and upon seeing him, she sucked in a breath.

"Oh my," was all she said as she rushed to the table. She started to get the funny glow that happens when she sub summoned an angel, and I knew she was going to try to heal him. In the meantime, I tried to pull the spine from my leg. It hurt terribly, but I managed to get it out and started to bandage myself.

"Where did you both come from," Greg started to ask as he helped me bandage my leg? "I didn't think anybody would come here to rescue us."

"I don't think they are here to rescue us at all," Bobby replied with a nervous voice before I could answer. "They are trapped here the same way we are."

"Not so," Jane said as she backed away from George. His wounds were closed, but Jane could not cure the poison. "He needs a healer. He is so week my healing almost killed him. However, I can get you all out and into the street. At that distance, they shouldn't come after you and you should be able to carry him back to town."

"Oh thank you, lady," both Bobby and Greg kept saying.

“I thought we would die here,” Greg finished.

“No, I can get you out,” she replied with a reassuring smile. She was very good at being persuasive and charming when she wanted to be, but something told me there was more to this.

“You keep saying you,” I said to her. “Don’t you mean us?”

Her face went serious. “No,” she replied. “I only have enough left to teleport four. I used the rest up outside and to heal George.”

“You can’t stay here, you will be killed,” I said back. “You take the boys out and leave me. I can fend for myself and with luck, you can get Henry or someone to come back for me.”

“I am not doing that Paden,” she responded. “You are going back and that is final.”

“Not on your life,” I said as I managed to stand. I hobbled over to her and looked her in the eyes. At first, she tried to look away, but something steeled her will, and she met my gaze.

“Paden, this is my job and my responsibility. I am not losing you here and that is final. You go,” she said as she dared me with her eyes to argue further. However, there was no way I would leave her to die alone.

"I will not allow you," I said back. I knew I couldn't stop Jane. All she had to do was touch me and think, and I would teleport to where ever she wanted within range. But after a few seconds of looking me in the eye, she relented.

"Just the boys then, but you and I are not finished arguing about this," she said as she turned to Bobby. "Bobby, get a blanket and two long poles if you can find them. We need a gurney so you two can carry your friend."

He didn't ask questions and ran around the manor looking for what he could find. In the meantime, Jane took a look at my leg and deemed it was well enough not to have to heal at that moment.

"At least this delay in the fighting has given us or magic back," she said, speaking softly, as we waited alone for the boys to find the items Jane needed. "When we have to fight we can make a decent showing."

I smiled at her. I couldn't help it. Even in the face of overwhelming odds, she was as calm as ever.

"Do you ever lose your cool," I asked?

She let loose a smile. “I try not to,” she said back. “In our line of work, it can get you into trouble.”

“It’s a good thing we know how to avoid that,” I said with a huge grin.

She smiled and almost chuckled, but the gravity of the situation held her back.

“Only you could joke at such a moment,” then she kissed me on the cheek.

“The best I get I guess,” I said before I could stop myself. I thought Jane would get angry, but she just looked away sadly before taking a big breath.

“Paden,” she started.

“You don’t have to,” I said as I stood up again and started looking for Bobby and Greg. I could hear noises upstairs like the boys breaking things, and I figured they were hard at work on something. “I know that you don’t like me the way I like you.” I just thought death was coming, so there was no reason to hold back my feelings. “I just thought...”

“That’s not true Paden,” she interrupted. “I do like you, a lot,” she said with a sad demeanor. I thought my heart would pound out of my chest, but then she went on. “But I vowed never to marry, and I don’t want to hurt you. You and I can never be more than friends."

It was a blow worse than the spine I had gotten earlier. I had to admit that I was already in love with her. We had been around each other now for almost three months. I could not go a day without thinking about her or wanting to see her. It was something that I knew in my heart was right, but she was refusing me and for the dumbest reason. She admitted she liked me back and yet still denied me.

"Why," I asked heartbrokenly? She could easily see my hurt on my face. She looked at the ground for a second before looking me in the eye again.

"Both of us are fighters Paden," she replied. "We put ourselves in danger at least once a month and most of the time more than that. Neither of us will have a long life even if we live through this. Then what if we have children how much worse would that be. I won't subject myself to that again."

I knew she was talking about her father. It was a pain I never realized haunted her this much. He had died when she was a child, and now she felt that if she got close to someone and had kids, it would happen to her. The problem was there was no way to argue against it.

"I understand," was all I said as I put my hand on her shoulder. She cupped my hand with hers, and I could see tears in her normally stoic eyes.

"We should go check to see what the boys are breaking upstairs," she said as she took a deep breath to calm herself. "I don't want to waste too much more time or the creatures may break through the walls. With as many of them as there is they might actually weaken the walls enough to dig through."

At that, she stood up and walked upstairs. I watched her go with a heavy heart before looking at the poor boy on the table. He was still breathing, thank God, but it was already coming shallower. If we didn't get him somewhere soon, he would die.

Luckily the boys came down again shortly after with Jane in tow. She looked as calm and detached as always as she carried two posts from the upstairs bed. The boys had the blanket, and they quickly laid it on the ground opened wide as Jane put the poles on it. Then they folded the blanket over the posts and placed George on the sheet.

Once the boys had finished, Jane looked at the boys. "Once you are out on the road, do not hesitate to go straight towards Normandia," she said as if she was taking a walk in the park. "Go quickly to the Cathedral and get Brother Sampson to look him over. He is the best healer outside of the King and should be well suited for this kind of work.

The boys shook their heads in understanding before each hugging her. Then Bobby came over to me and handed me his hand. "I will never forget either of you," he said with sorrow. "May the light always shine on you."

I knew he knew just what our staying would probably mean, and I was glad he cared. I took his hand and patted him on the other shoulder with my free hand. "Just get Gregory to the cathedral so that it is not in vain."

"We will," Greg said as it was now his turn. Then the two young men grabbed the gurney and waited on Jane. She glowed again for a brief second as she called another angel, then she touched Bobby on the shoulder, and all three of them were gone.

"Now it's your turn," she said as she looked at me. "I have enough left to get you clear."

"It won't do you any good," I replied. "I will simply try to come back."

She looked me in the eye with a pleading stare before looking away and giving up. "You're a fool, Paden," she said to me as I walked over to her and sat down beside her. She had taken a chair from the table and was now sitting. I did the same. "There is a good chance we will die here and I wish you would leave. Do it for me."

"It is for you that I will not," I said as I touched her hand. "Besides, it can make it till midnight won't you get your powers back?"

"Yes," she said with a smile. "But at the rate, they are devouring this house that probably won't happen." It was true. The creatures were dissolving the walls with their stomach juices and sucking the liquid out of the house. It was already brittle. A few more hours, and they would probably breakthrough. Once they did, we would be hard-pressed to escape.

Still, I wasn't going to give up without a fight. "Still, two of us are more likely to be able to hold them off than just one of us. If we can hold off then we might have a chance."

"You know if I ever was going to marry I would hope it would be someone like you," she said as she squeezed my hand and put her head on my shoulder. "You are a very good man Paden."

"You should tell that to my old warden," I said with a smirk.

This statement seemed to surprise Jane again, and we spent the next two hours talking about my past. I had never told her about my teenage years. I finally revealed to her that I had been a roaring drunk as a teenager and had gotten into so many fistfights that I had spent two months in a labor camp. My last fight was so bad that I almost killed the man I was fighting by the name of Howard Marshall.

I revealed to her my Masonry background and my old master Larry Osmond. I even let her know my father was an old blacksmith in Durin.

“I had assumed your history with The Masonry Guild because of your group’s name,” she said with a smile. She was still uniquely calm, but there was sadness in her voice. “But I didn’t know you knew some smith work.”

“I can shoe a horse,” I said with a grin. “But don’t expect a new mace.”

The truth has she already had a new mace from the last time we had worked together as she had to replace her old one. The new one had a hollow metal shaft and had fewer flanges causing it to be more durable and inflict more damage. Still, she got the point.

“I just didn’t realize just how talented you were,” she said back with a smile.

We smiled back at each other for a few more moments before she started to sing. It was a lovely lament, and it was hauntingly beautiful. Even without instruments behind her, Jane could make a song magnificent. However, she didn’t get to finish.

The creatures had been weakening the north face of the house for probably days, and now it seemed as if there was nothing but sawdust keeping it up. Finally, it wasn't strong enough to hold the creatures' weight, and the first one fell through.

I knew this was a problem, and I struck out with my ax. It was a good hit, and it died before it could shoot off a spine. However, the legs of another were starting to come through the new hole, and it wouldn't be long before we were chest deep in trouble.

I attacked, as did Jane. We kept pushing the creatures back out the hole, and they tried to climb in, but soon the animals just opened up more holes, and we had to put a shield up against it to keep the spines out.

After about 20 minutes of this, the inevitable happened, and the wall started to cave in. The cave-in would have been a disaster, but it happened just slowly enough for Jane and me to grab the shields and head up the stairs. The roof caved in then, and we knew the falling beams killed a few beasts with it, but now there was a hole large enough for many creatures to pass through. There was now no way to keep them out.

We set up our shields at the top of the stairs, feeling lucky that the walls here were still strong, and the stairs would funnel them at us two or three at a time. However, we would only get one shot off each before they came upon us, and then we would have to use magic and hand to hand.

The creatures didn't take long. They seemed to know where we were even without eyes. Soon they were pouring up the stairs almost like they had been pouring out the silo. Jane and I shot our bolts, exhausted our magic, and had stood our ground for several minutes before what was inevitable finally happened.

In her fatigue, Jane made a mistake, and her shield fell forward. It landed on the closer beasts, but it gave several others the chance to shoot. Three bolts hit her before she could do a thing, and if she hadn't fallen back away from the stairs, she would have died right there.

I admit I panicked. Seeing Jane fall was like a knife to the heart, and it was all I could do not to lose it entirely, but I did make a mistake. I dropped my shield as I ran to her. I, too, was struck again, this time in my ax arm, and the pain was scorching. However, Jane was my only concern. I grabbed her quickly and, with my draining strength, dragged her to the nearest bedroom. This bedroom was the one the boys had been in, and they had torn the bed to pieces. Still, there was the staw filled mattress where they had left it, and it was the only safety we had left. I propped it up against the far wall and dragged her behind it.

Once there, I did get a chance to look at her wounds. One was in a shoulder, another in a leg, and the other the right breast. None alone would have been lethal, but I didn't know how fast the poison would work on her, and she was already starting to weaken to a point she couldn't move.

"I can still save you, Paden," she said pleadingly. I could already feel several animals probing the mattress and trying to find a way around. "Let me save you."

"No," was all I said. Jane reached for me, and I thought she would send me away, but when her hand touched, she smiled weakly.

"You are still a fool," she said, and then she passed out.

Now many people say it is better to be skilled than lucky. I say it is better to be both. That day we were lucky. The first creature had just started getting past the mattress on the right when I heard what sounded like human feet coming up the stairs. Seconds later, I heard chanting, and the creature nearest me was hit by an energy blast and slammed it against the wall to my right.

I almost screamed with joy when I heard a human voice and saw hands grab the mattress to move it away. There stood two fully armored warriors looking down on us and looking over the situation. One wore a rust-red armor, scaled like dragon's scales. The other was wearing what I could only describe as a tree. Then it dawned on me. The red suit was dragon scales, and the other was a tree, but with the poison coursing through me, I couldn't comprehend what was going on. Then I was lying in the street looking up at my saviors.

“They will need a hospital Noty, get them out of here,” the man in the tree armor said.

“As you wish Master,” Noty replied. “But what about the problem, we need to drive away as many of the creatures as we can.”

“Once the curses are removed they will leave on their own,” the Master said. “But I will clear out as many as I can to avoid several Mobs forming. I don’t know what will happen when they disperse as even I have never seen anything like this.”

“The fighter’s weren’t joking. This is a whole new level of fungus,” Noty said again as he looked down at me. “I would call it a Bloom if you don’t think it inappropriate.”

“Works for me,” the master said. If he was smiling or serious, it was impossible to say. Both had masks on, and I couldn’t read their face. Plus, the venom was now working its evil, and I could hardly move.

“Be careful John,” Noty said with a stern voice. He sounded my age our younger, but I still wasn’t sure who he was. “Someone went through a lot of trouble to make this happen. If that druid is still around you may be in trouble.”

Then I thought I was dreaming. Several trees started to move towards the house, and the man in tree armor replied. "I am always careful my pupil, don't forget you need to be too. Get them back quickly and then come back here. I may need you to help finish up."

I honestly don't remember much more. I passed out just about when Noty got me into a cart, and the next thing I remember, I was waking up inside the Cathedral. Standing near my hospital bed was my team, Greg and Bobby, and Keith and Betsy Monday, Bobby's parents. Maria and Eddy were chatting everyone's ears off, as usual, while Bobby kept pace with the other two. I was glad to see Maria and Eddy not fighting, so I kept my eyes closed for a little while and collected my thoughts.

I listened to them for some time before opening my eyes and saying, "you guys are noisy enough to wake the dead."

The reaction was instant. Immediately everyone was by the bed talking to me at once and congratulating me on surviving. I honestly didn't feel like it was something to congratulate me on. I figured my rescuers were the real heroes, but the Mondays seemed to think I deserved some credit for their child's rescue.

I was also glad to see that Jane was sleeping soundly in a bed nearby. George was also in the one next to her. It seemed that everyone survived in this crazy event, and I said a silent prayer of thanks that it was the case. Then I spent the next few minutes explaining what happened and getting congratulated for nothing all over again.

Still, the Mondays said I was heroic and kept offering to give me a horse as a reward. I refused for a long as I could, but in truth, it would be months or a year before I could afford the horse they wanted to give me. I finally relented before Jane opened her eyes, and the cycle started again.

On the other hand, she accepted a horse with pleasure and then donated it to me before letting her know the Mondays had given me a horse already. The Mondays didn't seem to care. They had plenty of horses to sell, so they were delighted to provide me with two. I felt guilty, but Jane said it was a gift well given, and there was no reason to be guilty. We had saved their child and though we would have done it for free, accepting a gift was good manners. The Mondays couldn't have agreed more, and so I accepted their offer.

It was also then that I asked about our rescuers. I had not had a chance to see who they were and wanted to extend my pleasure, and thanks to them. I couldn't give them a horse, but I was willing to work for them for free for any reason.

It turned out that the man in the dragon scale armor

was none other than the Prince of Broma. It made sense. The man in the armor was slender and tall. The prince during the festival had been the same. Plus, everyone in the kingdom knew that the royal family were all mages and clerics. Still, being rescued by the prince seemed to be a tremendous honor, and I reminded myself whatever he needed, I would do at the drop of a hat, till this day that offer stands.

The other man was his druidic master John the druid. I knew nothing of druids but got a lesson fast from Jane. They are a cross between priests and paladins but deal mainly with the connection of man, God, and nature. It was the paladin like sub summoning that got us out of the house and the priestly powers that made John's armor. When Henry the Grand Protector came in to check on us, I also found out that evil Druidic magic had been the source that made the bloom happen.

Someone left two evil relics in the silo. One attracted spiny funguses, and the other repelled their predator, the blue hornets. That, combined with the grain in the silo, caused the bloom to happen almost overnight. The farmers didn't realize the problem until the spiny fungus had run them off the land. Yet, since nobody believed the numbers they talked about, the situation was left unchecked too long.

Still, the prince and the druid were said to have cleared them out, and everything was soon back to normal. All that was left for me to do once everyone had left was to sleep and heal.

## *Story 5*

# *First Contact*

There are some moments in life you never forget. Beauty, awe, and majesty being frozen into your mind till it is permanently a part of you. My first vision of Jane was such a moment. Even on my death bed, I imagine that moment will be as clear in my mind as any I have ever had. But some memories stick around for other reasons. Horror, shock, and disgust forcibly being shoved into a memory that lingers long after you wish it would depart. This story deals with one of those.

Work had been going as planned. We were already close to halfway through the second month of the year. It was Francesco the 12th, and my group and I were back on a role. We had completed three quests already, and I was finally close to Brawler rank. In truth, I had managed a small group without it. Yet it was a milestone, and I was anxious to achieve it finally.

With that goal in mind, we had taken most of the challenges offered to us. So when the job had come out to clean out the sewers, I had jumped at the chance.

Now, this might seem like a crappy job, all puns included. And it is true they only gave it to lower-ranking groups. However, they didn't give it to any low ranking group. The team they gave it to was always the one they felt most probable to succeed and most likely to become a household name in Normandia. With that faith in us bolstering our confidence, we had spent all day down in the sewers hacking our way through Rous's and funguses of every shape and size.

"That makes three for me," Maria said with a grin as she stood over her third Rous kill. The Giant rat would have given her fits just a few weeks before, but Maria had toned up and improved. It was just another thing that made me proud of my team that day.

"It's not fair," Johnny said with a grin as he wiped off his goblin fork. He too had killed a Rous and was now in stable third place behind Maria and I. "Paden keeps firing spells at them and you have your bow. This is only the first one you have killed with your sword. I think they should only count if you kill them hand to hand."

"You're just whining because you are getting beat by a girl," Maria said back as she batted her eyes teasingly at Johnny. Some men would have blushed with such an attractive girl teasing them that way. Not Jonny. He took it in stride.

“Damn right,” he replied with a mischievous grin. He was now more accustomed to the group, and his light-hearted nature was beginning to show. “Though being beat by you sounds like an interesting proposition.”

Everyone laughed, except Maria. She just turned scarlet. She was comfortable when she was doing the flirting, but her shy side took over when someone flirted back.

“Well you’re all being beet by me,” I said in reply. “I have four and there is very little sewer left for you all to catch up.”

“You don’t count fearless leader,” Johnny answered. “You’re using magic. No wizards allowed.”

“I agree,” Maria said as she helped gang up on me.

“No comment from Eddie,” I asked as I looked at him? “I can’t believe you won’t defend your leader.”

“I think we should only count based on style points,” Eddie said with a grin. He only had one, so style points would be all he could get. That got a laugh from everybody.

We were all having fun. It had been a good day, but the count wasn’t accurate anyway. We hadn’t counted the number of moving fungi and Xeroid beast the team had killed. If we did, there was no comparison. Jonny and Eddie had made most of the kills while Maria and I kept them supported. When rats came into view, I put Maria and myself in the front to give her some experience. Maria had started to keep count of the Giant Rats, and now everybody was in on it.

"So how much more," Johnny asked as he flexed for a second? The flow-through wasn't tight but being underground that long did make one feel claustrophobic.

Bromans called the tunnels in the sewers a flow-through. They are tunnels with a channel in the center. It allowed sewage flow away from the city and into human-made lakes and swamps that catch and filter the sewage.

Each flow-through has a walk area on each side one man wide. The channel is the same width. Three people could walk shoulder to shoulder in the tunnel and have enough room to fight.

We had been down in the Normandian sewers for almost the entire day. It was a testament to the city's size as Normandia needed at least 20 channels with numerous offshoots and maintenance corridors to operate smoothly. Yet it contained 24 for redundancy.

"Half a flow and we get to go home," I said with a stretch of my own. I couldn't wait to get the stink off me. The last section of Flow 24 was all we had left.

"And some hot mead," Eddie said with a sigh.

"That reminds me," Maria said as the boys started to lift the rouses into a float-barge, we had brought with us. The float was similar to a canoe that the maintenance workers would use to get materials or carry out large debris. We were carrying out the bodies of what we killed so other creatures couldn't feed off them. "You promised me last week to tell me why you don't drink."

"That is a question I have been wondering about myself," Eddie chimed in with a grunt. A rous could weigh as much as sixty pounds, and lifting one took some strength.

"It isn't that much of a secret," I said with a shrug. "Jane knows."

"I'm sure Jane knows everything about you," Eddie said with a smile and a wink. Had it been accurate, I probably would have laughed. Instead, it just made me grumpy.

"Jane is a proper lady bonehead," Maria cut in. "You shouldn't insinuate..."

I didn't let her finish. "Enough Maria, you don't have

to defend Jane's honor. Her honor will never be in question." The statement came out a bit harsher than it should have. I hated that Jane had made a vow never to marry, and my voice carried that frustration with it.

"I thought you two were sort of an item," Johnny said as he put his rouse in the canoe.

"I wish," I replied. If there was one way to ruin an excellent mood for me in those days, it was to talk about me and Jane's relationship. I decided to change the subject, "but I thought the lot of you wanted to know why I don't drink?"

"You two doing that bad," Eddie said. "Must be her vow."

"What vow," Johnny asked?

"Jane has this stupid notion..," Eddie started to reply. However, just then, I spotted something further down the flow and held up my hand for silence. It seemed to be tall and had at least two limbs coming out of it. It was dark down there outside of our lantern light, so that I couldn't see it that well.

My first impression was that a human was down in the sewer with us. Still, it moved wrong. It seemed stiff and sluggish. Not the fluid motions of a human. I concluded it must be another Xeroid beast. They are a fungus creature with four vines growing out of them. You could mistake one for a human in the dark, poorly lit areas like this, at certain angles.

Seeing danger coming our way oddly relieved me. Now I could easily change subjects and get the group off me and Jane's relationship. "We may have company. Get the rest of the rats on the float so we can haul them back," I ordered. I kept my eyes on the movement down the tunnel. It seemed to be moving slowly, but it also seemed to be coming in our direction.

Jonny and Maria looked down the hallway as they picked up the third dead rat I had killed and together put it in the float. Eddy, too stared down the tunnel.

"Is that a person?" Eddy asked. I heard the rat get dumped into the float, but my attention was on the shadowy figure walking our way. It was already close enough to listen to it sloshing through the 2 feet of sewage water it was walking in. For some reason, it was making me very nervous, and my hair was already on end. I didn't like it.

"Not unless they're hurt," Maria said. She had also picked up and the funny movements of the approaching shadow. Yet, the appendages I thought might be vines did start to look like arms as it got closer. Something was wrong!

"Get the lantern Eddie," I commanded as I grabbed my

spear and signaled Johnny. "Johnny is with me. Maria, keep your bow ready. Eddie, open up the lantern. I want to see what that is."

Eddie did as I asked, and he shined the light down the tunnel. The light reached our target, but only barely. However, it did give enough detail that I was now sure it was a human, and SHE looked hurt!

"Johnny," was all I said as I started to rush down the tunnel. Fear for the lady shot through me, and I could tell Johnny felt the same. He didn't need any further messages. He, too, could see the figure of a young lady on unsteady legs and in nasty bloodstained clothing. How long she had been down in the sewers, I did not know. What we thought we knew was that we needed to get to her. We should have taken a better look.

I had just about reached the wretched sight when the wondering girl looked up.

That moment will haunt me for the rest of my life. When I think of what evil someone can do in this world, that young ladies mutilated body always appears in my head. Clear and crisps as I saw it that day in the lantern light.

What must have once been a young lady was now nothing more than a butchered body. The bloodstained clothes and horrible gaping wounds told the story. Something or someone had killed the poor girl and then made her walk the world as a corpse!

Her clothes had hidden her wounds when her head had been down. Now that it was up, a gap appeared in the clothing. You could now see the mangled ribs as someone had torn open her chest, which had exposed her organs. They had cut open her neck, and her tongue was missing. They had even pealed her scalp away from her skull. It was a terrible sight!

I almost screamed. I felt the panic much like I had when I had fought the skeletons in the Stone Heart Cave. However, I held it back.

I came to a quick stop and signaled Johnny just in case he didn't notice. Then the creature looked at me. Its one remaining eye looked right into my mind and flood it with thoughts of death. Then it opened its mouth as if to scream. The silence of the scream being as terrible as any audible cry could have been. Then it charged.

I steeled myself, forcing my panic down and readying myself for the fight that was coming. I could not flee. I was wading in sewage and didn't have anywhere to go. Plus, the creature might catch me from behind, and I would then be in trouble. Instead, I planted myself in a forward stance with shield up, and spear arm cocked and ready.

In such a stance, most creatures would try to change their angle of attack. The Zombie did not. She didn't even slow down as she hit the spear and ran right up its shaft. Then she hit the shield, full force. I was lucky that it had been the body of a young lady around Maria's age because anything larger might have knocked me off my feet.

I tried to remain calm and pushed out hard with my shield. The creature clawed and ripped at my shield, my helm, and my eyes. Yet it couldn't do much with my shield in its chest and my spear in its guts. Then Jonny came up with his weapon and started to help.

He had modified his goblin fork from the original weapon. Instead of a noose on the back end, he had put a bar mace. This mace was a useful weapon against this kind of foe. Now he was using it by smashing at its back with the powerful weapon.

Each hit staggered the beast and tore huge gashes into its flesh. Still, it kept coming. I couldn't even get my spear back out of her as she wouldn't stop pushing forward towards me.

I decided I needed to change tactics and took out my ax. If the bar mace was useful, the ax was ideal. It honestly had the effect I wanted, and with each swing, I managed to take another large section out of the undead horror. But like most zombies, massive damage was nothing more than a flesh wound.

Even when Maria and Eddie joined in, the creature kept coming. We hacked off one arm and half of a hip before things started to change. With four fighters and no weapon of its own, the creature couldn't win. We pummeled the undead beast till it finally succumbed to our attack. After a few heart-pounding moments, we gave it its second death. This time it was for good.

"Where the hell did this come from," Johnny asked as he looked down at the dead body. He seemed to be the only person not affected by the tortured girl. The rest of us looked like we might lose our lunch any second. Maria did.

"Hell may exactly be where," Eddie replied with a sour look. He had seen enough and turned away.

"Something horrible happened to this lady," I said, transfixed on the body before me. The damage we had done was massive, and it was now hard to see where our weapons had landed, and those of her killers had. Still, there was no doubt in my mind the young lady had suffered horribly before her death. Something in my gut told me this was the truth. "We need to find out what. Eddie and Maria, go top side. Eddie go get Jane. Maria, you get guards. We will guard the body."

Maria and Eddie didn't have to be told twice. They both got torches out of the float. Then both quickly turned back the way we had come and disappeared down the flow-through. That left Jonny and me in the dark sewers with one lantern and a previously walking zombie. I admit. I was nervous.

I pictured hordes of these creatures coming out of the gloom and dragging Johnny and me into their ranks. Such a terrible fate was the stuff of my nightmares. I was beyond thrilled when Maria came back.

She had brought four guards with her, and they looked ready for a fight. Luckily the Zombie was down for good and hadn't brought friends.

We proceeded to get the body onto a dryer part of the sewer and inspect it further with better light. It was even more apparent that the damage to the body had been massive even before our fight. Yet what was more heartbreaking was that one guard was positive that much of it had happened while the girl was alive. He didn't elaborate on how he knew. He just said he was confident and left it at that.

Finally, Jane arrived, and the look on her face said as much as the look on mine must-have. Disgust couldn't even begin to describe it. I had gutted another man while fighting. It was horrible and something I would never get used to, but this was something on a whole new level. The fact there were monsters in the world capable of this made me sick.

"We may be able to find out more if we take the body back to the cathedral," she said as she too examined the body. "Henry could probably tell us what the last few moments of her life were like and give us a hint at who killed her."

"Are you sure she was killed Jane," Maria asked? "She could have just been raised by someone evil and collected all the damage fighting."

"No," Jane said as she stood up from where she had been kneeling next to the body. Tears were in her eyes, but the calm, professional voice that Jane was so good at keeping was all that came out. "The amount of damage the body must have had before this battle would have been enough on its own to kill a Zombie of this level. No, she was killed, and I expect slowly."

She didn't explain, and nobody asked. Even the ordinarily talkative Eddy and Maria were silent. The sight was just too terrible.

Jane then started to lose composure and had to look away as she shed a few silent tears. I tried to put my arm around her, but she gently brushed me away. Ever since we had told each other how we felt, Jane had done everything in her power to remind me that she had vowed never to marry. It was frustrating because I needed her to comfort me too.

"We need to identify the body," The one guard said. "If Henry can do that then that is where we need to go."

Jane wiped her eyes, then looked at the guard and shook her head yes. Then two guards put the body on a float and started back towards an exit. Jane then looked at me.

“You should get yourselves out of here, clean up, and rest. I will find out what I can and then come get you when we know more,” Jane said as she put her hand on my shoulder and brushed her hair out of her face. She had a sad smile, and I could tell she was angry with herself about brushing off my comfort attempt. It had been another thing Jane had been doing lately. She was throwing mixed signals about us. “I will need help finding the culprit once we know more. I will ask the guild to let you help me when the time comes.”

I shook my head yes and signaled my group that we were leaving. There was no need for words. A pleasant day had turned into a mournful night, and I knew I would be hard-pressed to sleep. I just hoped Henry could get us the information we would need, and somehow we could serve some justice.

We reached the guild several hours past sundown, and I was never so happy to make it to the baths. I must have sat there until midnight as I tried to wash away more than the grime. I looked like a prune by the time I was ready to leave, but the images of the day didn’t wash away like the filth. Even with my eyes open, the horrible disfiguration of the young lady was all I could see.

It bothered me to think anything could do that to another person. What kind of monster could kill in that manner? What type of animal!

Those thoughts also kept me imagining the last few

moments of the young ladies' life. What fear must she have felt? What pain and torment? The idea had my stomach feeling ill, and I knew there was no point in trying to sleep. I finally decided I needed to learn more, so I left the baths and headed for the Cathedral.

The night air was chilly as spring nights often are. The moon was a day out from full, and my path was well lit. It made the walk easy. Had it been any other night, it would have even been enjoyable.

I reached the Cathedral soon enough and was surprised to see Johnny standing near the entrance. He was chewing tobacco and staring at the night sky. He saw me as I came up the path and nodded at my approach.

"I thought you would be asleep by now," I said as I got close. Jonny smiled at me before spitting into a small bucket he had sat next to him.

"Not a chance," he replied before taking a deep breath and looking up at the stars again. "I have seen a few zombies before, but this one was different." Johnny had seemed the least affected by the body. Now it was apparent that he was just better at hiding it.

"How do you mean," I asked? I had never seen a zombie before that day and was curious about the differences.

“The goblin priests we use to fight would raise zombies from time to time,” he replied as he took his eyes off the stars and looked at me. “But they usually raised the bodies of dead comrades. This body looked like it was tortured before being raised. I don’t see what the purpose was for whoever raised it.”

I didn’t know. I knew very little of such powers back then and didn’t feel I could guess. All I knew is the girl was tortured, killed, and then raised. The only thing important now was finding the culprit and ended its ability to do so again.

“Has Henry learned anything yet,” I asked after a second of us both looking at the stars?

“Yes,” Johnny said before spitting tobacco one more time. “He learned her name is Stacey Russell. She is the daughter of a local merchant and has been missing for two months.”

“Poor thing,” I thought out loud, “too young.”

“17,” he answered in reply, an age that was way too young.

“Anything known about her disappearance,” I asked.

He answered by looking me in the eye and saying, “only two other things. She disappeared on a full moon and that she is the fifteenth girl in Normandia to do so in the last two years."

"None have been found," I asked, surprised?

"Not one," he answered.

Neither of us said a word for a little while longer. Then I decided to go inside and find out if there was any more news.

"Thanks, Johnny," I said as I patted him on his shoulder and started inside. "I am going to see what else I can find out. You should get some rest."

"I will wait for Maria and Eddie to come out," he said. I was surprised to hear they were there as well, but proud of my team's empathy. "There is a full moon tomorrow and I don't want Maria to be the next missing girl."

That thought sent a chill up my spine. Maria was only slightly older than Stacey had been. She was the right age for the culprit. I couldn't imagine what I would do if I found Maria in the same state as Stacey.

"You're a good man Johnny," I said as I walked past him and into the chapter. He replied with a sad grin before spitting into the bucket and looking up at the moon.

Maria met me first. She was sitting on a bench just inside the foyer reading a book. She looked tired but had spent some time in the baths like the rest of us. I could still see a little pruning on her fingers.

“Couldn’t sleep either,” I asked as I came over to her and sat down.

“No,” she said with a weak grin. “I thought I would be stronger than this.”

“Nobody should ever be strong enough to dismiss what we saw,” I replied. She leaned into me with a smile, and I put my arm around her shoulders. I was starting to wonder how much damage this experience had on the team. I knew we would probably have to take some time off after this.

“She was my age,” Maria said in response. “I can’t imagine what she went through.”

“I am trying hard not to try,” I responded. Then I got up. “Where are Henry and Jane?”

“In the healer’s quarters,” she said back.

“And Eddy,” I asked?

“In the chapel praying,” she said. “Apparently he knew the family and Stacey.”

That was not good news. I did not know how well Eddie knew Stacey, but if she had been a good friend of his or more, this could be hitting him hard.

"Then I will go talk to him," I said.

"Better wait," Maria said in response. She looked concerned. "He took the news a bit hard. I think there was a relationship between him and her and he is upset he wasn't able to recognize her earlier. Jane seems to think he will need time."

I just shook my head in understanding. "Then I'll go to Jane. I want to know what they have found."

She shook her head and smiled at me. I smiled back and walked on to find Jane. The whole situation was getting worse, and I wanted to make it end. There was already a feeling that if I didn't do something, I would never drive Stacey's image out of my head. I couldn't imagine what Eddy was feeling.

I sought Jane at the infirmary, but the priest was already there and told me they had left. He suggested I visit the kitchen, so I walked into the basement and went to the large dining area the Cathedral had there. I found Henry, Jane, and about six other paladins talking.

"Welcome Paden," Henry said as he waved me over. "I would have thought your group would be resting by now."

"Not easy to rest," I replied. Henry didn't ask me to elaborate on why. Everybody knew why.

"Rest will be important," Jane said in return. She smiled at me as I took a seat, her hand instinctively brushing back her hair. "We must hunt tomorrow."

"Tomorrow night most likely," Brother Washington said. He was a paladin of third-tier level 3, and he was considered very powerful. It made him a Paladin in rank and the eighth-highest member of the Cathedral. I had seen him many times before when I had visited Jane. I was not surprised to see him at this meeting.

"It will be our only way to find the killer if you are right," Henry replied to Washington. "We will not be able to tell who is infected until the moon rises."

"What is the theory then," I asked? I realized I was coming into the conversation late.

"Werewolf," Bob Johansson said. He was another high ranking Paladin at tier 4 level 2. Only Henry at tier 4 level 3 was more powerful. However, both at tier 4 were Grand Protectors.

"Aren't those very rare," I asked back. There were many cursed forms of humans, but werewolves were not common in Broma. There was a cure, and it didn't take long to drive the demon out if found.

"Very," Henry replied. "But there must be something in that order here. Why else do woman only disappear on full moons? And the mutilated body would fit."

"Have you ever seen one master," this was asked by William Rodmen. He was the only priest at the table. His rank was pretty low. Only a tier 1 level 2, he was nothing more than an Alter Initiate. However, the priest always outranked Paladins of the same tier. Therefore he would be the same rank as Jane, who was tier 2.

"No," Henry replied, "Though my master has seen many." That was no surprise. I had heard Henry's master was none other than Dillon O'Connell himself. The head of the Church of Broma had seen much more than werewolves. Legends about him had him even killing demonic dragons, a creature I thought at the time didn't exist.

"It's a big city," Brother Washington replied, "and the creature has been at this for two years. But if it isn't a fully realized werewolf then there is no explaining how we have missed it this long. I suggest we inform the guards and the guilds of the problem right now and start a full wolf hunt."

"Do werewolves normally raise the dead," I asked? I knew of a few legends about werewolves. None included raised dead.

“No,” Henry replied, “not unless they are fully realized and then they don’t need to wait for the full moon.”

“Then we should be looking for something else,” I said, stating what I felt was unmistakable. Whatever had killed Stacey might be working in the full moon, but it was also raising the dead. Pointing this out, of course, didn’t sit well with Brother Washington.

“Not necessarily,” He quickly replied. “It is possible that something has control of the werewolf. They are lesser demons. A high powered Malokian priest or Vampire may very well control one.” Of course, Brother Washington was reluctant to give up on the werewolf angle. It was his idea.

Other more powerful dangers, of course, sounded a lot worse than just a werewolf. This whole conversation gave me the chills, and the clerics were talking as if they were speaking about the weather.

“This is all speculation,” Bob said back while shaking his head. “We do have a responsibility to protect the city. But Paden has a point.” At this, several people looked unhappy. Henry and Washington both made faces. They liked the idea and weren’t ready to let it go.

Bob continued. “We are speculating that this is a

werewolf. But it could really be anything or anybody with a full moon fetish. If we spend all our time on this we would have to delay several other urgent missions. I mean, Brother Washington and I were leaving in the morning on a call. We cannot ignore a call from God and that would leave you shorthanded by two more. You don't have the men."

"But if it is a werewolf?" Washington asked. "The whole town could be in trouble if that curse spreads."

"What if it is a dragon or Minotaur?" Bob replied, a bit heated "or a Vampire trying to throw everyone off with the full moon?"

"Ridiculous," Henry said back. "No vampire would wait a month between feedings. It would weaken them too much. Besides, there were no marks on the neck or body to suggest prolonged feedings by vampires."

"It was just an example. But what if we are talking simply a serial killer," Bob replied. This subject must have come up before.

"We've gone over this. I have never heard of a serial killer doing this kind of damage to a body." Henry said with disgust. "Plus there is the full moon connection. Serial Killers don't wait that long normally and their frequency increases as they kill. Plus there are the bight marks."

“Giant rats in a sewer explain those,” Bob fought back. “And just because something isn’t common doesn’t mean it isn’t possible. There was the serial killer in Oxford who only killed on cloudy days.”

“One example out of dozens,” Henry bit back. “It proves nothing.”

“It proves there are other options,” Bob said. He was now starting to get red-faced, and the two highest-ranking Clerics at the table seemed to be letting their egos get in the way. It was not a good showing of clerical patents and understanding.

“Obviously we have several possibilities yet and must not pigeonhole ourselves,” William said as he looked calmly at his two superiors. He was young and outranked, but he was calm even in the most challenging social situations. He had become a priest for that very reason. It had helped him to gain a lot of respect despite his low rank. “So what do you plan we should do Bob?”

“I say let’s get the guards to put posts at each of the sewer entrances and exits tomorrow night and see if anything comes forth. If there is a werewolf we can have Jane and Paden there with a team equipped with silver. They can then catch or kill the beast and we have our problem solved. If it turns out to be nothing more than a man the guards can then get him. In this way, we have not wasted valuable resources on chasing something that is not there.”

"I would rather waste resources than have another young lady butchered Brother Johansson," Henry said, letting him know he didn't like the plan. However, he kept his voice respectful.

"And how about wasting resources that could be curing the plague in Lake Settle or the Bloom epidemic that is sweeping southern Broma," Bob replied, also coming back down to a normal tone. "We don't have the manpower, Henry. We have other urgent business."

It wasn't easy to sway Henry most of the time, but Bob made too much sense. The problems in the rest of Broma were killing people almost every day. I hadn't heard of the new Blooms, but I had heard of the spreading epidemic. These were huge issues. One killer who would kill once a month or two was not as high on the list as epidemics that were killing every day. It made this a hard decision and is why being a leader is tough. "Agreed," Henry said, defeated. "We will try your plan Bob; with any luck, it will solve the problem. At any rate, it is probably the best we have. There is just too little to go on."

"Exactly," Bob replied with a smug smile. He liked it when his argument won and didn't hide his pleasure well. He started to stand. "We have a plan, and Jane with Paden's help should be enough."

"I hope so," Henry said, "but my gut still says we should do an all-out search. I just hope I am wrong."

"Your gut has been wrong before," Bob said in reply, "Let's pray that it is once again."

"I certainly will Bob," Henry answered. "I certainly will."

After that, the meeting broke up, and everyone started to go their separate ways except Jane and me.

"Working together again," she said. Her voice was warm, but she didn't smile or look me in the eye. She had been a little harder to talk to since we almost died in The Bloom. However, we would be working together again, and I respected her too much to let it affect our work.

"It does," I said, making sure I smiled at her softly. Just because she had vowed not to marry didn't mean she had promised not to feel.

"Well, I suggest you get some sleep then," She said as she looked me in the eyes and smiled. It was a direct response to my smile, but as soon as she caught herself doing it, she looked away. "We need to get up in the morning to tell the family. Then we will be on standby till something happens."

I nodded in agreement, but she didn't stick around to watch. She had a nervous step as she walked away, and soon she was out of sight, heading up the stairs. At that moment, I thought our relationship would never be the same. I was regretting ever telling her how I felt.

I woke up the next day, well before sunrise. It had been paltry sleep. I just had a series of recurring nightmares all night, as Stacey Russell's ghastly face haunted my dream. I kept seeing her silent cry over and over again, just as my mind would let go to sleep. It was jarring, and I would bolt awake with a scream almost to my own lips and sweat pouring down. It was a miserable way to sleep. I woke up very sore, very tired, and wishing I had other things to do that day other than hunt a butcher.

I got changed and went out to find my group. It was going to be a long day, and I wanted to give marching orders to them. It wasn't ideal taking on a new quest when we hadn't gotten sufficient rest from the last one, but we couldn't help it. Time was not on our side, and we needed to be ready that night.

I went to the room Johnny and Eddie had picked out as their own and found both of them up. Johnny was sitting up in bed talking to Eddie, but Eddie was almost fully armed and ready to go.

"I see you're ready early," I said to Eddie as I entered. He looked more tired than I did. If Stacey had haunted me, she had probably tortured Eddie.

"I couldn't sleep," he replied. He was finishing his last boot, and I could see his sword belt sitting next to him. "I have to go out and do something."

"Jane and I are going to go to The Russell's Shop today and let them know. I think it would be good if you came too, Eddie. You already know everybody," I told him as he finished his shoe and grabbed his belt.

"Thanks, boss, but I am going back down into the sewer," he said. "We never finished flow 24 and I want another look at it."

I had forgotten in the confusion that we never went the full length of the sewer. It was a matter that had completely slipped my mind, and I felt like a fool. How could I forget such a thing? However, it was probably way too dangerous for Eddie to be going down there alone.

"Eddie," I started. However, he cut me off.

"You can't stop me, Paden, I'm going."

"I was just going to say take Johnny and Maria," I lied. He looked earnest, and I knew I wasn't going to be able to stop him. However, with Maria and Johnny, at least he would have some backup.

He looked surprised. "I thought you would try to stop me."

"No, you need this," I again lied. Besides, in a way, it was true. If I had been him, I would probably feel I needed this too. “You will be in command just do me a favor and listen to Johnny and Maria from time to time. I don’t want your emotions getting in the way of your mission.” I couldn’t stop him, but maybe I could temper him a bit.

He took a deep breath and looked over at Johnny, who was staring at me like I had killed his mother. His face stated he didn’t like this whole idea. But he too took a deep breath and shook his head in agreement. “Give me some time and I will be ready Eddie,” he said as he threw off his covers and got up. “It seems I am destined for the sewers two days in a row.”

“I’m sorry Johnny, but I have to go,”

Johnny then smiled at Eddie. “If it was me in your situation I would have to go as well.”

I was proud of the two of them. Eddie and Johnny were starting to become friends, and I like what the team was becoming. If only Eddie and Maria could get along.

I reminded them not to forget Maria, and then I left. I made my way down to the front office, where Gregory was at his post as usual. I told him of my assignment, and he put it down as official. Then I headed out to find Jane.

I didn’t have to go far. Jane was getting off Splash at

the stables as I walked up to get my horse. She was dressed in her official robes and wasn't armed except for her nightsticks. Our first mission that day would be to talk to Stacie's parents. It would require tact, not tactics, compassion, not force. I felt odd in my armor and ax. Still, I was representing the fighter's guild and thought it best if I looked the part.

"I am glad to see you are up early," Jane said. She smiled at me and brushed back her hair even though she had it in a very nice tight braid.

"It was hard to sleep," I said as I entered the stable. The stable boy had just gotten up himself and was walking over to take Jane's horse. He had not gotten the sleep out of himself as he dragged his feet a bit. It probably was a bit of a relief to him when Jane said she would be riding out in just a few minutes and when I told him I would get my horse myself.

"Which horse are you taking Paden?" Jane asked. I had two now, Onyx, my black Warmblood, and Slate, my grey. Both were good horses, but I thought Slate would be better today. She was a five year old with a great temperament. Even though her training was to be a warhorse, her character was calmer in the streets. Onyx was a fiery beast that could be hard to control in a crowd. It was safer to ride Slate when in town.

"Slate," I said. She just laughed. She had been there the first time I road Onyx. Had she not caught him with Splash, he would have galloped off after throwing me. She knew I still didn't trust that horse.

I got out Slates gear and put it on her. They kept Onyx in another stable where they housed the males. They never mingled the horses unless owners requested it, and it limited the accidental births. I was happy about this. I wanted to bread Onyx and Slate eventually and didn't wish to have cross breading.

Soon I was sitting next to Jane as we road through the city. I marveled at the difference in the horses. Splash was a big male mustang, but Slate outweighed him. She was nearly 300 lbs larger and had longer legs. Yet there was an air about Splash that made him seem the more impressive beast. He liked to walk with a bit of a high step and kept his tail erect as if he was in a dress parade. It was funny to watch, but Jane insisted his training never included this. He just liked showing off, and it netted him a crowd where ever we went.

It was no different that day when we arrived at our destination. We hadn't dismounted for three seconds before four people had come over to look at the Paladin's horse. It was a sight to behold as they looked him over and made a fuss over him. It took several more seconds before anybody even notice the real warhorse next to him. Then it was Slate's turn to be looked over.

Broma was a land of horse warriors, and Broman's loved their horses. However, we brushed off many questions people asked us and simply asked the oldest guy in the group if he knew where we could find Mr. or Mrs. Russell.

"I'm Jack Russell," a middle-aged man said who was still looking over Splash. The rest of the group started to walk away as it was obvious the horses were not for sale. "This is a fine pony. Hardy and strong, I bet he has a clever disposition as well."

Jane loved to hear praise on her horse. It was like music to her ears. "He is a very clever horse, but not as modest as he should be." Splash whinnied at the same time as if he disagreed with the statement. The coincidence produced laughter from all of us except Jane that shot Splash a scolding look.

"So what brings you to see me," Jack said as he came around to the other side of Splash and took my hand then Jane's. He was a middle-aged man with hair that was already grey. His face had some wrinkles already, and his nose was a bit misshapen as if it had been broken and then set poorly. However, he had a winning smile. His eyes, however, seemed distant and sad. He was hiding pain, and I knew exactly why.

"Let me guess," he continued. "You are here to buy your first pottery together for your new house and came to the finest dish and flatware store in town."

We blushed, and his face lit up. He must have thought he hit the mark as both Jane and I showed a lot of embarrassment from the statement. However, Jane was quick to catch herself. She then passed a hand through her hair and look at me through the side of her eyes for just a second.

“No,” she said. Her voice was steady, but she had already started to put in the compassion she needed for this job. “We are actually here for other reasons.”

He looked at us for a few seconds when his mind seemed to realize that I was a fighter, and she was from the church.

“Official business form the Fighter’s Guild and the church,” He asked. His smile was gone in a flash, and you could see the fear already taking everything else’s place.

“You may want to come inside and sit down,” I said. It was not my first time attending one of these meetings. Ozzie had made sure I understood this part of the job. I knew what the reaction was going to be.

“You found Stacie,” he said. It wasn’t a question. There was no need for one. The looks on our faces told everything.

“Late yesterday,” I replied. There was no point dragging it out. If need be, I could carry Mr. Rusell in. However, he was emotionally strong. Time had steeled him for this. It was apparent he had been expecting this news.

“Dead,” he asked? It was the last bit of hope in a man who knew the truth. I just shook my head to confirm he was right.

He just shook his head in reply and started for his shop. His eyes showed he was already in the stages of breaking down, but he held it together long enough to get his assistant to man the store and to take us inside and up into the house above.

We hadn’t made it five steps into the house when we heard, “dear is that you?” The voice came from the kitchen, and Jack’s wife came out, rubbing a morning dish with a towel. She took one look at her husband’s face, and one more at Jane and me, and the plate hit the ground.

“Oh God!” was all that came out as she broke down in tears. Her husband came over, and his resolve finally broke.

“They found her,” he sobbed as they both cried. “She’s gone.”

Telling a family, they lost a warrior is one thing. But telling a family they lost a young daughter to a senseless crime. To this day, I don’t know if there is a worse emotional feeling. I could feel tears running down my face as I watched the sorrow unfold before me. The pain was immense and terrible, and there was little we could do to help.

However, the church had trained Jane for this, as Ozzie had taught me. She, too, was teary-eyed, but she knew the Russell's would need to sit. Jane had walked over to the table and taken a chair from it. Then she moved it behind Mrs. Russell, who instinctively sat down.

I quickly followed the same example and moved a chair right beside her for Jack. He, too, sat down, and the two continued to cry for some time after that.

Jane and I sat quietly for a while, as the couple shared their grief. It was during that time we heard someone running up the steps just before the door flew open.

Now everyone knows what I think of Jane's beauty, but she is not the only beautiful Broman woman. At that moment, through the door, came another such woman. She was just about Jane's age with a similar figure and blond hair. The only two real differences were the height. Jane was taller and more muscled, while Heather had a soft and delicate build. If Jane's beauty hadn't already been planted in my brain, who knows. Maybe Heather may have been the one who had been frozen to my memory.

"They found her," she asked as she barged in? Both parents looked at her as the tears that had almost stopped started pouring again. Then they reached out to their remaining daughter. She bound across the room and knelt between her parents. They all started to cry all over again.

It was some time after that before Jack finally spoke. “I am really grateful you two came to give us this information,” he said with the crying finally subsided.

“We are sorry for your loss Mr. Russell and can only pray that some solace can be found in the fact that she is now with our Lord God,” Jane said with a compassionate smile.

“We thank you for your prayer,” Mrs. Russell said in reply.

“Is there anything we can do to help,” I asked? I had learned that one of the best questions you could ever ask was if you could help. It always helped a family to know someone cared.

“Can you tell us how she died,” Mrs. Russell asked in reply?

Jane and I looked at each other for a second before Jane answered. “It is probably best you don’t know the details, but I will tell you she was murdered.” Jane’s eyes never looked up from the table. I could see the tears she had in her eyes as well. I reached out my hand and put it on hers. She grasped mine back firmly. Her compassion was another trait I loved in Jane.

The family didn't seem to be taken back by the statement. They must have guessed the truth after all this time missing.

"And the killer," Mr. Russell asked? It was a fair question, and I hated I had no real answer yet.

"We are searching for the killer," I answered. It was true. Eddie and the rest of my crew were looking for him. "My best men are on it as we speak."

"I'm sorry if we haven't gotten your names yet," Mr. Russell asked? If he had looked middle-aged before, he now looked like he had aged ten years. I felt sorry for him and his family. I couldn't imagine such grief.

"I am Paden Lambert," I said. "I run a fighter's guild group called The Fighting Quoins. This is Jane Journeyman, Paladin, and disciple of Broma's Church, and a good friend of mine."

They smiled at us as both parents tried to wipe the tears out of their faces. Heather did the same as she looked at me.

"Are you the same Paden that stopped the attempted thefts of the Relics of the Sun," Heather asked?

"With a little help," I said as I looked at Jane. Jane smiled back at me before releasing my hand. Her eyes then looked at Heather, looked at me, and then back at Heather, and I thought I saw a bit of a smile.

“We would have never stopped them without your help,” Jane said back in reply. “You were instrumental in stopping the robbery.” I could have argued that point, but it wasn’t the place.

“I’ve heard of you as well,” said Jack. “You’re also the one who caught the crooked guard and fought two Ogres single-handedly.”

It was funny how stories got out of hand, but again there was no point in arguing at the time. It was best to nod and let it be.

“So how many men do you have working this case Paden,” Mrs. Russell asked?

“All I have,” I said in reply. I didn’t want to tell the grieving family it was only three. All sounded more impressive, and it wasn’t a lie. I wanted them to feel we were doing everything we could. “It is being led by Edward Koffing in my absence.”

“Eddie,” Heather said as I watch all three of them perk up with the name. “You mean Richard’s boy, Stacie’s old boyfriend?” At that, she got off her knees and dragged a chair over to where her mother was. Then she sat down again.

"The same," Jane replied.

"They grew up together Stacie and Edward," Jack said with a smile and a tear. "I always thought the two would get back together." You could see his mind drifting to that thought, and it brought more tears to his eyes.

"He has taken it hard himself," I replied. "He was the first one back at the investigation this morning. His determination is great and I know he has the skills to find the killer."

"You'd better find him before I do," Jack said as a bit of anger started to show on his face. "He deserves to rot in hell."

"Jack!" Mrs. Russell said, a bit shocked.

"He does mother," Heather said in response. "I'd kill him too if I found him."

"Heather, you shouldn't talk that way either," Mrs. Russell said back. "Stacie's gone but putting blood on your hands won't bring her back."

"More importantly," Jane said. "The suspect is dangerous and may not be captured or killed easily. We would ask that the three of you let us handle this. We will bring the killer to justice."

“I will pray that you do,” Mrs. Russell said in return. It was incredible how morally strong she was. In her shoes, I would have railed murder and death on the killer, yet she had the strength to seek only justice. I would learn Brandy was a devout person and a good woman. It was not in her to fight or kill. That is an amiable quality, even if it is one I could not follow myself.

We stayed for almost an hour after that, talking to the family and listening to stories about Stacie, Edward, their family, and the superb pottery and plates Jack made. The whole time Heather kept looking at me and smiling. It was a weird feeling, and I could tell she felt odd about it too. It seemed she found me attractive, and I her, but she could see I had feelings for Jane. Plus, we were talking about her sister’s death, and the whole atmosphere itself made it feel wrong.

I felt a bit relieved, and a lot drained when we finally left.

“Heather likes you,” Jane said as we mounted the horses outside.

I felt instantly guilty about the whole thing. I had already told Jane I loved her, and getting looks from another woman felt almost like cheating.

“I didn’t notice,” I lied.

"You should have," Jane said with a smile at me. "You kept staring back at her."

We started to ride away, and I was glad none of the Russells were there to see me blush.

"As I thought," Jane said with a mischievous grin.

"You know I couldn't date her Jane," I said. No point in beating around the bush. I saw what Jane was doing.

"Why," Jane asked? I looked at Jane, and I could see Jane wanted me to think of the idea. It made me mad.

"Why," I answered back? "Are you serious?"

"Paden, you and I..." she didn't finish. I didn't let her.

"I don't care," I yelled back. One passerby looked at me like I had just sinned. After all, Jane was wearing church robes.

"You should," Jane said back. "You shouldn't spend your life lonely."

"Neither should you," I bit back.

"We went over this Paden," Jane said back. "I made a

vow at the altar. I cannot break it."

"It was a stupid vow," I replied angrily. I couldn't believe I was having this conversation with Jane.

"You don't even know me that well Paden," Jane started.

"Bull shit Jane," I replied. Now my voice was carrying. I wouldn't be surprised if the Russells could hear me even though we had traveled a block already. "That is just a load of crock."

"Paden," she yelled back! "Watch your language."

"Why the Hell should I," I screamed. The look on her face spoke volumes. She was as frustrated as I was. It was amazing that just moments before, the two of us had been consoling a family through a time of great grief.

"I can't deal with you right now," Jane said as she spurred Splash into a trot. "You're just impossible."

I watched her ride away, and the sight made me angrier. I was mad at myself, at her, and the whole damned world. The nerve of her to try to pawn me off on someone else! It was just infuriating. I almost ran someone over, and I screamed at them to get out of my way. The poor lady looked like she was about to run when I did it, but I didn't notice. All I wanted at that point was to go to the guild. Then I would wait for a report from the guards or Eddie.

The sundial had moved two a quarter till dusk when Eddie came in. Eddie was exhausted, as were Maria and John, as they had searched the entire sewer with no success. There was nothing else down there now. We had done our job, and it was clean.

"We even searched the walls," John said. He had a bath towel in hand already, and I knew exhaustion had him. "Nothing. We cleaned out the entire sewers."

"I expected as much," I replied. Whatever we were searching for wouldn't be down there. There would have been more bodies.

"Do you expect that the culprit will even bother with the sewers again," Maria asked? I thought about it for a minute. The lack of other bodies was probably the key. What if it had found its way into the sewers as the Rous does? Maybe we were looking in the wrong place.

"Eddie, was there any large holes in the sewer grates where a person could get through," I asked? Why hadn't I thought of this before? The culprit could be just outside the city walls or in a building near an entrance. We were looking in the wrong place! Stacie's Zombie could have just entered the sewers when we found her. We were dumb.

"Several," Eddie said as his tired face lit up. He was now on the same page. "I'm an idiot!"

"Don't beat yourself up," I said in return. "I think we have all been too tired. I need you to get washed up and get some rest. I think we will try again right before dark. A plan is forming."

"You know I am a bit surprised Jane didn't think of this either," Maria said as an off statement. They were good friends, probably best friends at this time. "She is usually so quick."

"Whatever," I said back harshly. It was uncalled for, but I was still mad at Jane.

Nobody answered back. My statement left surprise over all their faces; then followed the awkward, nervous movements before Eddie broke the silence.

"We need to get ready for tonight. We have a lot to do."

With that, the group got up and left me. I was glad they didn't ask questions. I would have lost my composure. I was still angry with Jane.

It was about an hour later that Jane came by. She was with Henry.

“We have a problem,” Henry said as he came in. Jane and I exchanged glances, but the look on my face made her look away. She didn’t even change her expression. A steady calm look like the world didn’t matter. Knowing as I know now, I would have realized she was trying hard to control her emotions. It was a curse of hers that she didn’t like to show she was human. But I just took it as her being cold towards me. It didn’t make my mood any better.

“The guards were with your men as they went through the tunnels. They know that the sewers are empty so they are pulling back on the number of men they are giving us tonight,” Henry continued. “We now really don’t have the men for the mission.”

“Doesn’t matter,” I said confidently but with a little bite. Jane’s presence was making me grumpy again. “My men found several ways in and out of the sewers that a person could get through. I suspect the Zombie found its way in the same way.”

“True, but I still suspect the sewers are a highway for our killer,” Henry replied. “He may not really be dumping bodies there, but how else does he kidnap women and then get them away somewhere private so quickly.”

“He would have an entire night,” I said in return.

“Maybe he just drugs them and carts them out of the city or to an abandoned house. I don’t see that the sewers are necessary.”

“You have a point,” Henry returned. I looked at Jane again. She was pretending not to listen for some reason. She still wasn’t looking at me. “You do have a good mind, Paden.”

I didn’t answer that. I was now also giving Jane the same reaction in return. It was admittedly childish.

“Makes tonight even more difficult,” Henry said with a huge sigh. “Bad enough we have few guards to help and no clue where we should be looking but we also have the problem of two best friends who are giving each other the evil eye.”

I wasn’t even listening to that intently. My mind was still on Jane, so it took a second to realize what he said. However, once it sunk in, I let it out.

“Jane is an impossible pain in the ass,” I said. It felt good getting it off my chest. I didn’t even notice Henry was glowing slightly. He must have known I needed calming.

Jane said nothing; she just looked at the wall on the other side of the room.

"How could anybody make such a stupid vow," I said in frustration? I saw Jane's fist, clench. I had hit the mark. Henry, on the other hand, started laughing.

"I don't see where this is funny," I yelled at him. It was dumb. I couldn't believe we were having this conversation.

"I knew this day would come," he said as he looked at Jane. "Jane, would you leave the room?"

She now looked hurt. There were tears in her eyes. What was worse was that I was glad to see them. I was relishing the fact I hurt her as if it was payback. She got up and left.

"I thought there was an issue when she stormed into the church and didn't even stay long enough to brush Splash. She looked mad enough to strangle someone."

"She could have fooled me," I replied.

"Everyone knows how you feel about Jane," Henry said in reply. Everyone knowing was a bit of a shock to me. Had she told everyone else? "What's more is the fact that Jane loves you back."

"And someone who loves you would try to pawn you off on the first woman who shows interest," I yelled back. It's funny how Henry could get to the bottom of anything so quickly.

“Is that what happened,” he said back with shock? “I would have thought even she knew better.”

“Stacie’s sister Heather showed some interest and Jane had the nerve to suggest I pursue her,” I said back. I was starting to calm. “Is that love.”

He took a second as he looked at the door Jane had left. Then after a few seconds, a devilish look came onto Henry’s face. It was brief, and soon he was back to normal. “For Jane, it makes complete sense.”

Then he looked me in the eye and became a bit serious. It wasn’t the normal Henry.

“Jane is a stubborn, complicated, and frankly confused young lady,” He started. “She has feelings for you of that I have no doubt. But she has made up her mind and there is nothing in this life that will change her mind.”

I knew that, and it was why I was hurting. It just sucked to hear Henry confirming my fears.

“She loves you Paden, of that I have no doubt, but she probably wants to save you the hurt of chasing the uncatchable. I don’t think she understood that whatever she did would hurt you. It was already too late for that. Probably too late for you the moment you laid eyes on her." He said that with a bit of a faraway look. Then he looked me back in the eyes.

"But I think she may actually be right."

"You don't mean that," I replied as my frustration started coming back.

"I mean it," he replied. "The vow is stupid. In fact, I have tried to tell her countless times that the vow would keep her from achieving her full potential. I am more convinced of it now than ever, but there is no more stubborn human in this world. You may wait a lifetime for her only to find she will never come over. No, there is no reason two people need to be miserable. You need to let her go."

I sat there, ready to argue. It was a terrible day and getting worse by the moment, but I didn't have the opportunity. Jane busted in with a scribe from the church. Both looked very concerned.

"News from the Russells," Jane said with a lot of concern. "Heather left this morning to bring Paden a message and never returned."

I was up in a flash. Heather missing was the icing on a terrible day.

“Worse, someone saw her being dragged into the sewers about twenty minutes ago. Two guards went in to stop them and met with Zombies. They were driven out of the sewers.”

“Not a werewolf,” Henry said as he too got up quickly. “We must act fast. It could already be too late.”

“We must go now,” I said as I grabbed my shield and spear. I didn’t have time to put my armor back on. That was stupid, but we had to hurry. “Do you two have horses?” I asked Jane and Henry.

“I have Splash but Henry just took a donkey over,” Jane said nervously. She was anxious to get going.

“Get Onyx Henry, he can be saddle quickly as I had him on standby. I have Slate ready to go and will go with Jane.” I said as I started for the door. “You,” I said to the scribe as I came up to the door. “My group is in the baths, let them know and tell them to hurry.”

With that, Jane and I were running full speed to the horses. We were outside and riding in a flash. Both horses were fast, but Splash was no match for Slate’s speed. She was genuine warm blood, and her long stride easily outpaced Splash. It was lucky Jane had mentioned which entrance we needed as we were running out of the building, or I might have ridden nowhere in my haste.

The night was getting dark, and a large full moon was already high in the sky, but I didn't notice much. The streets were still alive and busy, and it was taking all I have to keep from running people over as I rode down Main Street towards Baker's district. The entrance I needed would be there.

I was a block in front of Jane when I arrived. Several guards were already there, cleaning up two more dead bodies of girls. Where these zombies had come from was beyond me, but they had come out of the sewers. This incident convinced me that Henry and I had both been right. This killer was using the sewers and coming in and out via the gaps Eddie had found.

I didn't wait for much of a report. I jumped off Slate and ran towards the sewers. Two guards tried to stop me, but a flash of the badge let them know I was here on business. I entered and started running down the stairs. There were two more guards there collecting a fallen comrade who had been cut down by the zombies. They had two torches, and I took one without hesitation. They looked like they would stop me, but I just pushed past and ran full speed down into the sewers.

I was lucky. I knew the sewers well after that night before and had a feeling I knew were to go. There was a larger room about two blocks further. If I were a murderer, I would choose there. They would be below the old bakeries that were closed down. Nobody would hear a thing there. It was a gamble, but the sewers were as large as the city. It could take half a day to search the entire thing, and we didn't have that time. The Russells had already lost one daughter. I'd be damned if they lost two.

I ran hard, but as my horse was faster than Jane's, Jane was faster than me. She caught up just a few turns before I got to where I was going.

"Where are you heading," she asked through her heavy breath?

I told her my theory as we now jogged. She didn't reply but started running as well. We bounded ahead when voices came floating up from the room we suspected. Jane came to a halt and told me to hold up. I didn't want to but reluctantly stopped.

"Kill her know Zack, they are coming," One voice said calmly as day.

"Why did you leave me, Stacie," another voice said. I assumed it was the Zack we had heard the other voice talk to. "Two of your sisters have been taken because you left."

I didn't understand. Stacie was dead, and this man would have to know that.

"Your power wasn't enough yet to hold that many girls," the other voice said calmly. "You need more power and this life will give it to you."

"Shut up Caesar," Zack yelled back. "She's mine! You already had your meal from her."

"It's not about the meal," Caesar said calmly again. "But she betrayed you, she is attracting other men, if you don't kill her now and teach her she will call trouble on us."

"Is it true, Stacie," Zack yelled? "Have you called more men? Are you still a temptress, after all I have shown you." The voice sounded genuinely angry and was getting louder. I was ready to get in there, but Jane held me back for a second longer as she quietly opened the door slowly.

"Please let me go," a crying voice pleaded. It was Heather. She was still alive, and this Zack had her confused with her sister. By this time, the door was half-open, and I was ready.

"Too late," Caesar said again as calmly as a stroll in the park. "They are here."

He'd seen us, so there was no more reason to be cautious. We burst in to see two men and Heather in the room. It was a square room with a deeper square pool in the middle. It was one of the central channel collectors where workers operated gates to control the flow.

The one I figured was Caesar was sitting with a relaxed air to himself on one of the grates on the far side. Meanwhile, the one I assumed was Zack had Heather on a walkway on the side nearest us. I didn't waste time. I charged at him, and he looked surprised and scared. He started running away from me while brandishing a long curved dagger.

"You bitch, you called more men," Zack yelled while back-peddling from me. "You evil Bitch!"

I had no idea what was going on, but I had to get him away from Heather, so I pushed forward. It would be no contest. I realized right away; this guy had no fighting skill. However, I should have been looking towards Caesar.

In a flash, Caesar had crossed the room, blown by Jane, and had shouldered me into the wall like I was a rag doll. I hit with a thunk, barely missing Heather. Yet Caesar was not done. He kept coming and picked me up by my neck with one hand and pinned me up to the wall. He wasn't a big man, nor did he look strong, but my feet were a good three inches off the ground. I had never felt such strength.

"Run Zackary, I will take care of the temptress and her evil minions," Caesar said as calm as day. Then he pivoted his hips, and I went sailing into the center of the room with a splash. I honestly almost drowned as it knocked the wind out of me.

I came out of the water just in time to see a fireball streak across the room and explode in Caesar's face. Jane was in the fight and was casting. It looked like the fight was over quick. Caesar started to scream in pain and contort as he caught on fire.

Jane didn't hesitate. She ran across the room with her mace in hand, and the heavenly glow around her intent on finishing off Caesar quickly. However, Caesar had a surprise of his own.

Just as Jane got close, Caesar started laughing and lashed out. He grabbed forward, ignoring her mace, and grabbed her by the shirt. He got a face full of flanged mace for his callousness, but it did nothing to stop him. With a flick of his hips, Jane went souring through the air just as I had a moment before.

I watched, stunned, as Caesar then seemed to dissipate into mist and come back together. Both the fire damage and the mace damage were gone.

"What are we up against," I asked Jane? She looked as stunned as I was.

"Death," Caesar said as a grin split his mouth and showed us his fangs. I knew then what we had stumbled into, and I knew it was beyond Jane and me.

"Jane," I said, knowing what was about to go down. "Get to Heather and get her out of here. I will hold 'it' off."

"He's mine," Jane said as she let anger get to her. "You can't fight this, but I can."

"Really," Caesar said with a sinister grin. "If I were you I would see just how far you can get before I tear you apart."

"Go," Jane yelled as she got to her feet and gave the room her full force light. It was impressive bright, but the Vampire only flinched.

"Bring it, Paladin," Caesar said. Jane didn't hesitate, and I didn't either. I ran for Heather, and Jane tried to block Caesar from us. It didn't work.

Caesar was quicker than either of us and much more powerful. He ran right at Jane and collided with her shield full force. Jane had good form, but she took the strike head-on instead of letting it glance off. It was all she could do to keep him from us, but she wasn't strong enough. The blow lifted her off her feet, and she went tumbling into the water again.

I knew I wouldn't have time to cut Heather loose from the bonds on her, so I changed directions and headed for Caesar. No point in pulling out the ax, and my spear was still against the wall where I had dropped it. All I could try to do was keep it busy till Jane was again on her feet. This battle was a fight to the death, and we had no weapons to hurt the beast.

I ran at Caesar as he stood there, laughing like a fool. I knew I didn't have the strength to tackle him, but I fainted as if I would. As I thought, in his overconfidence, he spread his arms wide in a jester that said, 'go ahead.' But that was not my intent. I switched to a spinning heel kick and caught him directly in the hips. On a normal man, I would have broken the pelvis. On Caesar, all I did was push him over, but it did give me a small chance to delay him.

I jumped on the creature, fearful that I was about to be torn apart in this attempt, but it would give Jane a chance to save Heather, and that was what was necessary.

I straddled the Vampire as it tried to get up and started to ground and pound. It wouldn't kill such a creature, I knew that much, but my hope was that it would slow it down.

It looked good for about three seconds. Caesar was surprised by my tactic. He obviously never had anybody foolish enough to fight him hand-to-hand. But he was immortal, and I was not. A few seconds of this foolishness was enough to really piss him off. In the blink of an eye, he grabbed my wrist and bucked. He was so strong that my hips went half a foot in the air. It gave him the ability to get his knees up.

I landed on them with my stomach, and I felt all

the wind go out of me. Then with inhuman strength, Caesar simply threw me off to his left and into the wall again.

Then it got up and started towards the ladies. Jane had made it to Heather and had cut her loose, but both were not ready for a fight, and the Vampire was now not playing. He ran across the room and grabbed Jane. He didn't throw her this time as he simply held her by the neck and started squeezing.

Jane had no chance, nor did Heather's brave attempt to get him to let go. She was slapped back into the wall for her effort.

However, Caesar did make one mistake. My spear was up against the wall he threw me against, and a spear is nothing more than a metal-tipped stake. I picked it up and ran straight at him, stabbing for his heart from behind. I missed. At the last second, Jane tried to save herself with a kick and made Caesar stumble. The stumble may have saved its unlife. I hit him two inches too far to the left.

The Vampire was shocked. I saw him look down to see three inches of spear tip sticking out of his chest. He knew he was in trouble because I was already pulling it out, and the next attack was not going to miss. He threw Jane down again and turned to face me.

However, I was ready now. I had my shield and spear back, and Ceaser obviously knew I could potentially kill him.

The two of us started fighting as I did everything I could to avoid his hands. Quick attacks that were hard to grab were all I could manage, and he was having trouble getting inside my range. However, it didn't last either. He knew his weaknesses and strengths better than anybody else. When I struck during one of our exchanges, he simply angled his body and allowed it to hit.

It would have been fatal on most other beasts, but on a vampire, it was nothing. Then Caesar grabbed the shaft and spun. Since I was holding on to the other end, I went flying, leaving the spear with the Vampire.

This was really bad. I felt my legs and arms burn from exhaustion and bruises. I even felt my breath coming difficulty from all the hard landings. It didn't look good, and now the beast had a spear.

Caesar started laughing. He knew he was winning. Jane was gasping for air, Heather was out cold, and I was shakily getting to my feet. I hadn't been in this much trouble since the troll in the Stone Heart Cave, but I hadn't stopped. I was going to fight this thing till my last breath.

I stood up and got my shield up. I had another plan. If I could hit my own spear just right with my ax, I could break it. This would give me a new stake to fight with. It was my only shot. Besides, Eddie and my crew were still out there, and they would be on their way with the guards. There was still a chance left.

“Pathetic,” Caesar said as he jumped into the water to fight with me. “The best this great city can produce? There has to be better than you two.”

“Don’t count me out yet,” I said, trying to be tuff. I hoped it would attract Ceaser to me. It worked.

“So be it fighter,” he said before charging. He stabbed forward, but I was lucky. He was no spearman. His underhanded attack was aimed at the shield, not at me. I had my chance and opened up my guard to allow the spear to pass by. Then I shut my stance and caught the shaft between my arm and shield, holding it fast. My next attack was at the shaft of the spear with my ax. It worked. His strength was so much, and the force on the post was so great that the blow shattered it.

He had been trying to pull it out when I hit it, so when it let loose, he went stumbling backward. I now had a suitable weapon again and an unarmed enemy.

I put my ax back on its loop and took the broken shaft into my fighting hand. By this time, Caesar had recovered, but he was now hesitant to attack. I also saw Jane picking up Heather. I knew if she left, I would be in the dark, but in the water, I could hear him coming. I had to trust in my skills and hope I would get lucky.

“Come on you piece of shit, let me show you pathetic,” I was hoping the taunting would lure him in and give Jane a chance to escape. It worked. He charged me, and the fight was on one more time. This time I was able to keep him at bay with my shield. I didn’t fight with the shaft as I was looking for an opportunity. I would be damned if I would let him take my weapon the same way twice. But my stamina was waning. Then the room went dark.

Jane had left, and it was now just up to me to stall the creature. I couldn’t win without light, but I could see him with sound. I was hoping it would be enough.

“So the Paladin has left you to your fate,” I heard out of the darkness. “She didn’t tell you what kind of vampire I am.” He was laughing now as if this was funny.

I heard nothing for a few seconds, and I figured he had stopped moving. I did the same. I didn’t know if he could see in the complete darkness of the underground. I had to hope.

Then his voice rang out again, this time from another part of the room. “The water won’t work in this case champion. I can move without causing a single ripple.”

This was terrible news. If Ceaser could move like that, I couldn’t fight him, let alone beat him. He could leave me there, blind as a bat as he went after Jane. Then he could come back to finish me off at will. I hadn’t felt fear like that in a while. I felt utterly helpless. What could I do?

Fear has a way of keeping the obvious away from you, but luckily it dawned on me. I am a mage! I had been a fighter so long I often forgot I could cast spells. I started chanting an easy spell Bio search. Caesar obviously knew what that meant, and I heard a splash. In his haste, he had forgotten to do whatever it was that allowed him movement without disturbing the water.

It was my break. I finished the spell just as the sound came closer, and I lashed out. It was a terrible shot, but it had the effect I would never have dreamed of. I hit him right in the right shoulder and pinned the bone in the arm and shoulder in such a way as he could not strike back.

He was now furious. What he must have thought was helpless prey was fighting back and causing damage. He stumbled back in a rage, forgetting to take the spear shaft with him. I still had it, and so could continue to cause him problems. I could see even in my exhaustion that the tied was turning. He was losing control as his frustration was getting the better of him, and any moment he was going to do something stupid. I had a feeling I could beat him.

He started forward again, but this time things changed significantly in my favor. The room light up bright as the sun. Henry had arrived!

The Vampire had been discomforted by Jane's light. He was practically burning from Henry's. He took one look at the Grand Protector and knew he could not take both of us.

"This isn't over battle mage," he said to me as he turned into a mist and floated through some grates and out of the light and room.

I stood there, huffing as Henry ran to me, followed by three guards.

"You ok," he asked me as he ran over?

"I had him, Henry," I said. It probably wasn't true, but I felt like I could have taken him. I had taken his best and found him wanting.

He looked down at my hand. It was holding the shaft with the broken wood part forward and the spear as the hilt. The spear had cut into the palm of my hand, but I hadn't notice. I wanted that beast. I hated he had just floated away.

"You don't look too bad but the hand will need looking after. In the meantime, I am going after that Vampire. Guards don't follow. It is a Draco and too strong for you. Paden get them out of here safely and then get Jane and come to help. I may need it."

“As you wish,” I said. I liked how Henry trusted me enough to come back, but I needed the break. I escorted the guards to the surface where Jane was sitting there with a recovering Heather.

“Jane, Henry needs our help. The guards should be able to get Heather home safely from here.”

Jane shook her head in agreement as the guards helped Heather up.

“Jane, Paden,” she said as she looked at me mostly. “Thank you, I could…”

She didn’t finish. She was too shaken up.

“I will come see you when this is over,” I said as I looked at her. I saw Jane’s face behind her. She looked sad but pleased at the same time. I felt a little bit of the anger I had before, but Henry was right. I couldn’t wait forever for something that probably would never be.

“I would like that,” Heather said as she came over and gave me a hug. She was soft and comfortable to hold, but I felt a bit guilty hugging her. Getting over Jane would take some time. Plus Jane was there looking. I felt so odd. “You kick their asses for me and my sister.”

“I will,” I said as she pulled away. “Stay safe.”

She nodded her head as the guards led her away. Then Jane and I delved one more time into the darkness of the sewers.

We searched all night, but we never found a trace of either Zack or Caesar. It was like they simply vanished. It was a terrible night for the most part, but we had saved Heather. Still, it was a small consolation to the family of the dead guard or the bodies of the girls that the guards had chopped down. They had gotten away.

Still, the hunt was on, and there was hope. There would be another full moon, so this was only the first contact. There would be others. We would meet them again.

www.ingramcontent.com/pod-product-compliance
Lightning Source LLC
Chambersburg PA
CBHW030619310726
48979CB00003B/797

* 9 7 8 1 7 3 6 8 3 0 0 0 0 *